MW01166691

# GOD
# BLESS
# FORTRESS
# AMERICA

# GOD BLESS FORTRESS AMERICA

## Henry P Mitchell

Writers Advantage

San Jose  New York  Lincoln  Shanghai

**God Bless Fortress America**

All Rights Reserved © 2002 by Henry P. Mitchell

No part of this book may be reproduced or transmitted in any form or by any means, graphic, electronic, or mechanical, including photocopying, recording, taping, or by any information storage retrieval system, without the permission in writing from the publisher.

Writers Advantage
an imprint of iUniverse, Inc.

For information address:
iUniverse, Inc.
5220 S. 16th St., Suite 200
Lincoln, NE 68512
www.iuniverse.com

ISBN: 0-595-23522-0

Printed in the United States of America

To the innocent victims who were killed and injured in the terrorist attacks on September 11, 2001, and:

- to their families who suffered the loss and impacts
- to the brave rescue workers who lost or risked their lives
- to the dedicated law enforcement and military forces that fought the War on Terrorism

# Contents

# Foreword

This is a work of fiction. It is based on a variety of factual information, events and historical figures. However, it also includes speculation, opinion and imagination. Many of the events in this work did happen and more could—but they don't have to.

# THE CELEBRATION

On the tenth anniversary of 911, America celebrated its security. As always, the 911 holiday was a solemn occasion. But this year, over one million people gathered at the Ground Zero Memorial for a commemorative event. It was the first time in many years that very large crowds were allowed to assemble in public places, so the people were thankful. It took a decade to build the Fortress at tremendous cost and sacrifice, but America was now secure in its belief that there would never be another September 11, 2001—ever again.

Once, by coincidence, simply the nation's standard emergency phone number was now adopted as a symbol of America's quest for security, and an annual tribute to all the casualties and impacts since that tragic day in history. It served as a rallying point as well as a remembrance. No one could ever forget, because America would never be the same. Although it was officially designated as "Patriot Day", September 11 became commonly referred to as "911".

Although New York City had become the symbol of the terrorist attacks and the initial focus of the traumatic impact, over the years all of America was affected. The sacred grounds of the World Trade Center would serve as a permanent monument of 911, but every city and town had changed. This was a different nation in a new world. Life and business returned to New York City, once considered the most popular and, arguably, the most important city in the world— now officially the financial center of the *Federation*.

America had been gripped with fear for a decade, but now that the Federation was established and stabilized, it provided freedom from fear. The American Federation is a strong, impenetrable Fortress State—secure, but isolated. America is still a democracy, but with restricted freedoms. It is still a world power; much larger and stronger than before, but no longer a world leader. The period of US world dominance that began with the fall of the Berlin wall on October 9, 1989, ended on September 11, 2001.

It was only a few months after the fateful attacks that most people began to feel that the war on terrorism would be an isolated and short-lived chapter in American history; like the Gulf War or the war in the Balkans. But it proved to be a major landmark in history that ultimately changed the geo-political landscape of the entire world and the very nature of American life—forever. The *Star and Stripes* now waves proudly as the banner of unification and security of the American Federation, spanning the entire Western Hemisphere, and stretching around more than half the globe. Few would have dreamed that such significant changes would occur to the world at the very beginning of this new millennium—and so quickly! But everything changes more rapidly in the 21st century. Communications are instant. News is available in real time, all the time, everywhere. Wars are television events. The 911 attacks were live on TV for all of America to see and indelibly print those unbelievably horrific images into their memory. Advanced technologies changed the nature and speed of warfare. Rapid technological advances routinely revolutionized the lives and expectations of people. The changing values of populations made people more impatient for results. It is not surprising that changes can occur rapidly in this 21<sup>st</sup> century world. But who would have believed they could be so dramatic?

Not everything moves quickly however. The "War against Terrorism" that was launched in response to the 911 attacks proved to be an undertaking that is now expected to last decades, not a few years as originally imagined. It took years to even begin to build effective intelligence networks for infiltrating and eventually destroying terrorist cells around the world. It took ten years to build the Fortress, but the terror and evil that evolved over hundreds—even thousands—of years could not be completely eliminated in such a relatively short span of history. As the American Federation celebrates its security, it also recognizes the price it paid and its continuing challenges. This is no longer the USA, and there is no turning back.

# 911: EVERYTHING CHANGED

Life was never the same after September 11, 2001. In response to the question of how many casualties were expected in the World Trade Center, the Mayor of New York said: "more than anyone can bear". Of course, those chilling words turned out to be so horribly true. After months of funerals with few bodies, America had to accept the thousands of fatalities and casualties that occurred in just a few short hours in New York, Pennsylvania and Washington, DC.

The attacks of 911 were on the *core*, the *icon*, of the American Heritage. New York City was the "melting pot", the "world city", and the "financial capital of the world". Washington, DC, and the Pentagon were more than just the capital of the United States. They were symbols of American power. This was the first and only other strike of war on US territory since Pearl Harbor. America was at war; a war unlike all others! 911 was the "Pearl Harbor" of the 21$^{st}$ century; another "date that will live in infamy". This was the first war for the USA with more casualties at home than in the military overseas. "We are in something different now than we have ever been before", said the Mayor of New York prophetically. America did not realize the real nature of the world around it. This was something that just "could not happen here".

4

What the President of the United States characterized at the time as "a quiet unyielding anger", led to radical change in the political philosophy of the nation. Terrorism reduced the entire population to a common level—a focus on survival and life. It does not discriminate between rich and poor, or black and white. The victims of the initial attacks came from 80 different nations, and also included 800 Muslims. It was not just an attack on America, or even the "West". It was an attack on modern civilization! The anger and fear bonded a nation together, and focused both its energy and resources on action and change; more dramatically than anyone would have imagined at the time.

911 was "apocalyptic terror". It was not just another suicide bomber or an isolated incident that killed innocent civilians. That had been going on for years all over the world, including in the United States. Terrorism was not foreign to the USA. There was the Oklahoma City bombing, the Columbine massacre, and the Unabomber, but it was still unacceptable to Americans. The terror of 911 was massive in size and scope, and inherently evil in nature. For the first time, the world witnessed the results of a sophisticated plan by a large network of terrorists. It was also the start of a new kind of war, with no nations or boundaries. It demonstrated, as the terrorists had intended, that America was no longer invincible. What the world did not realize at the time was that it would lead eventually to a true Apocalypse!

Much has been written about the terror of the 911 attacks and the aftermath of the early years that followed. But a retrospective after a decade has passed reveals how much has changed; not just for America, but for the entire world. This was not about a single incident or a regional war. It was the culmination of many years of hate and rage that exploded into an era of global terrorism that ultimately had to be confronted. 911 was the "wake up call". America responded, and the world would never be the same again.

# THE ENEMY

Who was responsible for these unprecedented attacks on America? What enemy was so powerful to have such a terrible impact on the world's leading country, and ultimately the entire world? It was an enemy unlike any that the United States had ever faced before. It had no nation. There was none of the traditional political or territorial aggression. America was the only "Super Power" and no longer faced the threat of attack by other nations. It was the model for democracy and freedom. Both fascism and communism were defeated by their own failures and American persistence. Tyrannical leaders were losing their grips on their restless, subjugated populations. America was relied on by most countries for economic and political stability. It was the enforcer of peace in the world. So who was this faceless, nameless, nationless enemy that dared to attack America?

To understand who the enemy is one must follow the trail of their development. They were not an indigenous people in a country that you could find on a map. They were everywhere—and sometimes they were nowhere. The enemy was not sophisticated in traditional military terms. Their weapons were usually simple, sometimes even crude. Their finances were limited, even meager. But their resources were formidable. They had an army of thousands—potentially millions—all willing to die for their cause. Their battalions were cells, dispersed in a vast worldwide network of fanatical terrorists. These groups of terrorists were linked, but not united. They shared a hatred of Israel and the United States, but had their own regional, political or ethnic priorities. The origins of the many diverse terrorist organizations varied in time and location. However, their paths often crossed as they helped each other in their common cause. One group, in particular, became the focus of attention after 911—al Qaeda. It had emerged as a global organization, building a record of major terrorist acts against the civilized world. International terrorism did not start or end with 911, but it would prove to be a turning point in history with Islamic fanaticism as the root cause.

## THE SOURCE OF ISLAMIC TERRORISM

Islamic terrorism certainly did not start with or was limited to Afghanistan and al Qaeda. And this was not a war with al Qaeda. It appeared to be "a war between civilizations"; Islam versus the western world. America became a symbol of a culture that was foreign to the ideals of Muslim fundamentalists. It did not happen overnight. There was a steady rise of Arab anti-Americanism during the last 30 years of the 20$^{th}$ century. The widespread hatred of America among Arabs was the result of many factors and events—some connected, some not. It seemed to start around the middle of the twentieth century, after the Second World War, when Arab states were winning their freedom from western/European colonization and when the state of Israel was created in 1948. This was essentially an international takeover of the Palestinian homeland. Arabs saw foreign Jews imported into Palestine to occupy and govern some of their most sacred land. This "betrayal" by the Western Allies was reinforced years later when America supported Israel in their wars with neighboring Arab states in 1967 and 1973. These wars with Israel proved to be humiliating for the Arabs. Israel then annexed occupied Palestinian territories and ruled them with what was perceived as "police state" control of 3 million Arab people. By establishing Israeli settlements in these occupied territories, the Palestinians felt that they had no homeland of their own.

The terrorist movement became visible to the world when Israeli athletes were kidnapped and massacred at the Olympic Games in Munich in 1972. The USA acted as an arbiter in getting Egypt, Israel and the Palestinians to agree to peace in the Camp David Accords of 1979. However, America continued to be viewed by the Arab world as a supporter of Israel. America aggravated its position over time by establishing a large foreign military presence in Arab states, and the sacred lands of Saudi Arabia in particular. Every time that the Israeli armed forces used both American weapons and military aircraft to fight and kill Arabs, the hatred for America grew.

The Middle East had been a hotbed of terrorism for over 50 years. Generations of Palestinians have opposed the State of Israel, and fought to regain a homeland of their own. The first Arab-Israeli war occurred in 1948 immediately upon the formation of Israel. And there was a war every decade since. In the meantime, terrorist attacks on Israeli citizens and military retaliation became part of a way of life in the region. The border wars with neighboring Arab states fostered terrorism throughout the Middle East. Since the United States was a constant supporter of Israel, it too became a target for terrorism. A variety of fragmented— even competing—terrorist groups developed. In the late '60s a Marxist organization emerged called the Popular Front for the Liberation of Palestine. But its support waned as communism lost favor, and the Palestine Liberation Organization or PLO became the dominant political faction under the leadership of Yasir Arafat. He had created the Fatah movement in 1967 as a paramilitary organization to fight Israel and gained control of the PLO in 1969. This became the "mainstream" of secular Palestinian politics. It was not a fundamentalist Islamic movement. But there were more radical groups. A small militant group was formed in the early '80s, calling itself the Palestinian Islamic Jihad. It developed a specialty in suicide bombing. The civil wars between Christians and Muslims in Lebanon that lasted from 1975 to 1990 devastated Beirut and created a Shiite Muslim "fundamentalist militia". Hezbollah was founded in 1982, and sought to establish an Islamic state and fight a guerrilla war against Israel's occupation of southern Lebanon. It was both a militia and a political party. As a Shiite Muslim movement, Hezbollah had support from Iran and Syria that enabled it to also help the Palestinians. Hezbollah gained notoriety in America as a terrorist organization when it was held responsible for the truck bombing of a US Marine compound in Beirut in 1983 that killed 241 US service personnel. Hamas, or the Islamic Resistance Movement, was established in 1987 as a Palestinian militant group in Gaza with both a social services role and a military arm. It developed a mutually tolerant relationship with the Palestinian Authority, but was often at odds with the PLO. It waged a campaign of terrorism in Israel through its military wing—the Qassam Brigades. Hamas obtained funding support from private donations as well as neighboring Arab countries.

Between Hamas, the Popular Front for the Liberation of Palestine and the Palestinian Islamic Jihad, there seemed to be no limits to the sources of terrorists and suicide bombers. Palestinian suicide bombers killed hundreds of civilians in a long series of individual attacks. They even had their own martyrs' organization. The Al Aksa Martyrs Brigades was formed in 2000 as part of the military arm of the Palestinian Fatah organization. With the support of the Palestinian Authority, it focused on attacks against Israel and specialized in suicide bombings. But it later declared that "American targets are the same as Israeli targets". The first uprising against Israel, or "Intifada" started in 1987 when 17 Israelis and 424 Palestinians were killed. Starting in 2001, there was a significant escalation of terrorist attacks in Israel—a second Intifada. But this time the rate of Israeli deaths increased significantly. Hundreds were killed and many more injured in what seemed to be weekly—if not daily—incidents. As Israel retaliated with aggressive attacks on the Palestinian Authority and suspected terrorist groups, the violence only increased further. Iraq even contributed to this escalation by offering payments that were the equivalent of $25,000 to the families of suicide "volunteers". Hamas was also "enraged" by the US war in Afghanistan, and began to target the USA in addition to Israel. Hamas had to be taken very seriously since it was known to have access to North Korean rockets. The "Qassam 1", which had a three mile range, was obtained through Syria and could be used by terrorists within Israel.

Egypt had also been a major source of terrorist movements and leadership in the Middle East for many years. Sayyd Qutb influenced a generation of Islamic militants and was executed in 1966 for plotting against Nassar's government. Anwar Sadat, who led Egypt into the Camp David Accords, was assassinated in 1981. Al-Jihad, also known as Islamic Jihad, developed as an Egyptian terrorist group responsible for both additional assassination and bombing attacks into the '90s. A number of Egyptian theologians established the radical Islamic Group in the 1970's, also known as Al-Gama'a al-Islamiyya. They later expanded and exported their militancy. In 1997 Egyptian terrorists from al-Gama attacked and killed 62 people in Luxor, including 58 foreign tourists. One of the founders of the Islamic Group, Sheik Omar Abdel Rahman, moved to the United States and set up camp in New Jersey, where he was ultimately convicted of terrorist plots and sentenced to life in prison. Osama bin Laden referred to Rahman, after his arrest for the plots against facilities in New York City, as a "martyr to the Islamic Cause". It was said that "if Rahman dies in prison, there will be a lot of problems in the US".

The Arab countries themselves were often their own worst enemies. Many were ruled by dictators and kings, even tyrannical Arab leaders who oppressed their people. The United States and its policies in defense of oil interests supported many of these perceived tyrants. The great oil wealth in the region went to the upper and royal classes. Most Arabs were an impoverished and uneducated people despite the riches around them. They resented the wealthy classes that exploited them, and the Americans who helped to keep them in power. There was a spread of "Islamic Politics" to take over the governance of countries. "Islamists", as they were called, opposed democratic, or royal, rule. Their objective was to establish states ruled by conservative Islamic law or "Sharia". Many of these militant Islamic groups failed in their attempts to overthrow the governments in their home countries in the '80s and '90s, including Algeria, Egypt, Syria, and Saudi Arabia. They then focused on western countries and the USA. In particular, they wanted to drive the US military out of Saudi Arabia and the Persian Gulf region in general.

The Islamic world was not united. There were long standing conflicts between Muslim sects. The Sunni dominated Afghanistan and Pakistan, and were the leaders of the Pashtun tribes and the Taliban. Saudi Arabia is also mostly Sunni. Iran, on the other hand is dominated by the Shia branch of Islam, or Shiites. The Shiites are a minority in Afghanistan and were persecuted by Sunni Taliban. Sunnis and Shiites could be found in each of the major ethnic groups in Afghanistan such as the Pashtuns and Uzbeks. So when they focused on their own world, Muslims often fought each other. But their common hatred of the "infidels" would bring them together to fight their "holy war". The Islamic world developed a self imposed cultural isolation from the West. It wasn't open to the ideas of others. The fundamentalists believed that focusing on the "true faith" would return them to the previous glory of the Islamic Empire.

During those last decades of the 20th century, there was also a resurgence of Islam, a religion and culture that had dominated that region and beyond 600 years earlier. One landmark event was the Islamic revolution in Iran in 1979, when the royal class was overthrown and a Muslim state was established. Religious fundamentalism gained political power. "Wahhabism", from the teachings of Muhammad bin Abd al-Wahab two hundred years ago, emerged as a popular puritanical form of Sunni Islam and spread to many countries. Inherent in their fundamentalist views was a rejection and animosity towards modern western civilization and its values. The strict Islamic doctrine emphasized an intolerance and hatred of non-Muslims. This culture that was foreign to Islam became known as "americanism". Religious schools or madrassas, produced tens of thousands of what were called "half educated fanatical Muslims who view the modern world with suspicion, and America as evil". A large portion of the population of Arab countries was young and impressionable. About 50% were under 25 years old. They were brought up with the new faith and hatred of America. Militant Islamic groups were encouraged, even inspired, by victories of the Mujahadeen in Afghanistan against the Soviet Union as well as the revolution in Iran.

There were also other wars during this period that resulted in the further erosion of the American image in the eyes of Muslims. The war and isolation of Iraq after its expansionist aggression of Kuwait ultimately hurt the poor population of Iraq. Despite America's military support of neighboring Arab countries, it was the US enforcement of sanctions and air patrols of Iraq that some felt helped perpetuate poverty, hunger and poor medical care within the country. This turned most of the Iraqis and other Islamic countries in the region against the USA. Also in Afghanistan, where the US helped in the defeat of the Soviets, America experienced a major setback in the aftermath. The abandonment of Afghanistan after the war left it exposed to a takeover by the radical fundamentalist Taliban rebels. The Jamiat Ulema Islam "party" helped the rise of the Taliban as a political force in Afghanistan. It was only several years later when the Taliban provided safe haven to al Qaeda terrorists.

So what drives Arab terrorists to be willing to kill themselves in the fight against Israel and the United States? It must be the 50 years of anger and humiliation for Israel's presence in Palestine, and for Palestinians living for 35 years under military rule in territories that were captured and occupied by Israel. This was seen "as a continuous reminder of Arab weakness". The significance of this self pity in relation to terrorism has been explained by a Palestinian psychiatrist in these terms: "shame is the most painful emotion in the Arab culture… producing a feeling that one is unworthy to live…The honorable Arab is one who refuses to suffer shame and dies in dignity." Palestinians and their Arab supporters were frustrated with the series of failed peace talks and the unfulfilled promises of Israeli withdrawal from Palestinian territories. The Oslo Peace Accord in 1993 was an agreement to establish a separate Palestinian state comprising the West Bank and Gaza, but it didn't happen. All Israelis were considered the enemy, and America was their protector. Anti-Americanism grew among Arabs as they watched Palestinians be killed by Israelis using American weapons. They also saw on TV the civilians killed in Afghanistan by American bombing. Arab hatred was reinforced by the continual TV coverage of the goriest images of Muslim casualties. The Arab TV network provided a totally biased and controlled perspective of what was happening in both Palestine and Afghanistan. It didn't seem to matter how many Afghans were killed by the Taliban and the warlords in the previous civil wars. All they knew was that America killed Muslims. Palestinians were willing to continue to fight Israel for their own state. They had adopted an Islamic perspective to drive their sacrifices: "Algeria had one million martyrs before they had their independence." This conflict was not going to end soon or easily.

## AL QAEDA

It was said that "If you kill Osama bin Laden, there are a hundred more like him to take his place". Who was this enemy and why was he attacking the United States? Of course, this was not the first time the world heard of Osama bin Laden or his terrorist group—Al Qaeda ("The Base"). They had been credited with a variety of attacks throughout the world for several years. He was a known threat, but unfortunately, greatly underestimated. Back in 1998, the United States failed to destroy, or even impact, bin Laden and his movement in response to their prior attacks when they bombed US embassies in Africa and a US destroyer in Yemen. Osama bin Laden had become a symbol of anti-Americanism. He was not a leader of an organized army. He was considered a hero and spokesman for many separate groups of Islamic extremists that used terrorism to fight "the devil". Al Qaeda developed as a global network of terrorists as well as an "umbrella" organization for other local terrorist groups to use for operational support. Thousands had been trained at terrorist camps in preparation for widespread attacks. There was a pool of hundreds of individuals in many countries willing to sacrifice their lives for the "cause". Martyrdom was considered the "highest rank" in the Islamic religion; an entrance to Paradise. America learned the hard way that you can't deal with people who are willing to kill themselves while taking the lives of others.

The origins of al Qaeda were the resistance forces, based in Pakistan, who fought in the war against the Soviets in Afghanistan. During the 1980's, the Mujahadeen Movement became freedom fighters for Afghanistan against the Soviet occupation. They were led and supported by Osama bin Laden. The pre-cursor leader to Osama bin Laden was Abdallah Azzam, a Palestinian operating in Pakistan. Bin Laden later added his financial support. The Soviet invasion of Afghanistan occurred in 1979, and they finally withdrew in defeat in 1991. The focus of al Qaeda then moved from the Soviets to Saudi Arabia and Egypt, and ultimately, to the USA after the Gulf War. Al Qaeda provided support to other local terrorist groups, such as the Armed Islamic Group in Algeria. They established training camps for terrorism. It was estimated that between 10 to 20,000 terrorists from over 60 countries were trained at al Qaeda "Jihad Camps". Abu Zubaydah, who was captured in Pakistan, was bin Laden's top Lieutenant responsible for training and managing the growing global network of terrorist cells. He screened and assigned terrorists and coordinated the plans for their attacks. Young men were routinely trained to blow up public and private infrastructure, to conduct assassinations, and kidnap hostages. A trademark of the Qaeda bomb making school was a simple timing mechanism driven by a Casio® electronic watch. This was not a sophisticated military operation. Its weapons were simple but its soldiers were committed. Their objective was terror, not conventional war.

The Islamic Jihad organization in Egypt merged into al Qaeda during the 1990s, a process that was completed in 1998. Their leader Muhammad Atef became Osama bin Laden's military chief. Bin Laden was the figurehead and provided the original funding source of al Qaeda. Under the leadership of Osama bin Laden, al Qaeda developed into a network of terrorists stationed throughout the world with access to substantial funds, not the least of which came from bin Laden's personal fortune and business interests. The Qaeda network spread throughout the Muslim world, from Algeria to the Philippines. Al Qaeda trained Arab terrorists were sent to Bosnia in the 1990's to help Muslims during the Balkan civil war. Of course, in the Middle East, there were also a number of other terrorist organizations that were well established prior to al Qaeda, and focused on the defeat of Israel and the return of Palestine to Arab rule. This included Hamas (Palestine), Hezbollah—"Party of God" (Lebanon), Islamic Jihad and the Muslim Brotherhood (Egypt). They shared al Qaeda's fanatical Islamic philosophy and hatred of the West. There were even sympathetic groups as far away as the Philippines, such as the Abu Sayyaf Group ("Bearer of the Sword"), the Moro Islamic Liberation Front and the "the Pentagon group" who were armed and dangerous rebels. They were linked to al Qaeda and known for their kidnapping of foreigners, including Americans, and beheading their hostages. Al Qaeda also moved into Indonesia where they provided money, training and foreign terrorists. A network of al Qaeda terrorists was built in Europe during the 90's and went relatively undetected. At the time, countries were focused on their own terrorist threats, such as the IRA in Ireland, the Basque E.T.A. in Spain, and the Algerians in France. Eventually, the visible emergence of al Qaeda led to a crackdown in Europe on international terrorists.

The world seemed to first learn about the Qaeda network as a result of the 911 attacks. But prior to 911 al Qaeda had been responsible for ten years of terror against America. In 1992 al Qaeda terrorists bombed a hotel with US servicemen in Yemen. The assassin of Mayer Kahane in 1992, the militant Jewish leader in America, was linked to Osama bin Laden. During 1993, bin Laden actively supported the killing of American soldiers in Somalia. Of course, their first attempt to bomb the World Trade Center occurred in 1993 resulting in 73 casualties including 7 deaths, but left the buildings to remain for their ultimate catastrophic demise 8 years later. During these early years, the Qaeda network began to develop and implement their terrorist plans without drawing the attention of law enforcement authorities. There had even been prior evidence of the bomb making and plans for the World Trade Center. Ramzi Ahmed Yousef, who was convicted as the mastermind of the first World Trade Center bombing, and who later planned to blow up American airliners over the Pacific, was found to have developed early plans to hijack airliners and use them as fuel laden missiles. He even told the FBI that "next time we will take them both down". This proved to be one of the early examples of unfortunate oversight by US Intelligence. In 1995 and 1996 there were car and truck bomb attacks in Saudi Arabia against US servicemen with hundreds of casualties. The truck bomb at the American military barracks in Dhahran, Saudi Arabia, in 1996 killed 19. In February 1998, Osama bin Laden issued a formal order or "fatwa" that it was the duty of all Muslims to kill Americans and their allies, including civilians and military. Then truck bombs attacked the American embassies in Nairobi, Kenya and Salaam, Tanzania in 1998 killing 224 people, including 12 Americans, and the rest were local Africans. There were also around 5000 injured. This led to the suicide boat bombing of the USS Cole on October 12, 2000 in Aden, Yemen that killed 17 US servicemen and wounded 30. These attacks got America's attention, but not enough to stop al Qaeda from its fateful mission. In fact, in anticipation of the US retaliation for the planned 911 attacks, al Qaeda assisted the Taliban in the assassination of Ahmed Shah Massoud, the Northern Alliance leader. This was a major blow to the anti-Taliban forces.

Despite these repeated incidents of terror, there were actually many attacks that were foiled. Plots were uncovered to assassinate the Pope, the US President Clinton, and Egypt's President Mubarak. Sheik Omar Abdel Rahman, the Egyptian Islamic leader in New Jersey, and his followers, were discovered and arrested for plans to blow up major landmarks and transportation infrastructure in New York City in 1993: the UN headquarters building, the New York Federal Building, the Lincoln and Holland tunnels, and even the George Washington Bridge. Rahman and nine others were convicted in 1995. There was also a plot uncovered in Manila that planned to blow up 12 US airliners over the Pacific in 1995. Ramzi Ahmed Yousef, who was also responsible for 1993 bombing of the World Trade Center, was convicted with two others. There were plans to conduct multiple terrorist attacks during the celebration of the new Millennium. Israelis celebrating in Jordon were the target of 22 terrorists who were convicted and connected to al Qaeda. Of course there was also the arrest of Ahmed Ressam, an Algerian extremist trained by al Qaeda and known as the so-called "Millennium bomber". He was captured at the Washington/Canada border crossing while driving a car bomb headed for the Los Angeles airport. The targets of terrorism were not limited to the USA. Al Qaeda plans were found for the bombing of London's financial district. There were plans for major bombings of the US embassy in Paris and NATO Headquarters in Brussels. The plans by Algerian terrorists to crash an airplane into the Eiffel Tower were foiled. When the Singapore cell of the Jemaah Islamiyah (Islamic Group) was apprehended, plots were uncovered to blow up US Navy vessels, airplanes, office buildings and the embassies of Israel, Great Britain and Australia in addition to the USA. The "shoe bomber", Richard Reid, who was caught on a flight from Paris to Miami, was linked to a cell in London and training camps in Afghanistan. Macedonia broke up a group planning to attack the embassies of the USA, UK and Germany. The local National Liberation Army of ethnic Albanian guerrillas was linked to Islamic terrorist groups from Afghanistan and Pakistan. In Rome a group of Moroccans were arrested when plans were discovered for an attack on the US Embassy by using cyanide to poison the water. There are a couple of lessons here. Terrorists *can* be stopped before they do their damage. But there were more of them and more opportunities than the law enforcement authorities can find.

There emerged a new generation of al Qaeda terrorists that did not fight in the Afghan war with the Soviets. Among them were a group of new extremists, called Takfiris, from Takfir wal Hijra (which means anathema and exile) or "Islamic Facisim" with its origins in the 1960s.

Dr. Ayman al-Zawahiri, the mentor of bin Laden and one of the key leaders of al Qaeda, was the chief ideologue of Takfir. These extreme terrorists were trained to blend into society to escape detection. They targeted Westerners as well as Muslims. The Takfiris gained popularity among al Qaeda cells in Europe. These proved to be the most dangerous of the terrorists. They were the "special operations corps" of the terrorist army.

What kind of damage do you think could be done by a group that has as many as 1000 people willing to die for their cause? How about if it was tens of thousands?! There was disagreement among some Islamic leaders at the time about the legitimacy of bin Laden's leadership and Jihad tactics. But there was no disagreement about the common hatred of America and Israel or the desired destiny of Islam. What was not understood was how powerful a weapon this loosely coupled network of militant fanatics could be.

So what was al Qaeda? It was not an army or a gang. It was a network of terrorist groups and a training organization, as well as a funding source for international terrorist acts. Al Qaeda had no direct connection to many local militant groups with specific local agendas, such as the Palestinians. Al Qaeda was, in some respects, a service organization, run more like a business than an army. It served terrorist groups from more than 20 countries with its training operations in Afghanistan. In addition to providing a comprehensive training program, it offered standard tactics and techniques that were proven effective. The recruits were also tested and indoctrinated as Islamic warriors. This was a fairly sophisticated operation that took years to build. The programs were formal and rigorous. Al Qaeda assembled an extensive collection of training materials. Many were obtained from American and Russian sources in the Soviet-Afghan war. There was also a lot of material available publicly, such as from gun and militia publications. They developed a cadre of experienced professional trainers, many veteran Mujahadeen fighters. The US and Russia would have to live with the fact that they trained the Trainers of al Qaeda! The training camps may have been crude in appearance, but they were functional. They provided adequate food and shelter along with weapons and training facilities. It was no small accomplishment to get individuals from very different backgrounds to work and fight together. Al Qaeda developed "standard terrorist soldiers" out of raw recruits from a wide variety of cultures, languages and ethnic origins.

The training, although standardized, was offered in a number of different forms. It was often tailored to specific or unique needs. There were actually several different types of trainees involved. Many were trained to be guerilla fighters. Like soldiers in a military, they learned infantry skills; combat, weapons, artillery. These were trained to serve in rebel armies, or in the case of Afghanistan, to fight the Alliance forces. Others were trained to be terrorists. They required different skills, and in many cases, needed a higher level of intelligence and fanatical commitment. Terrorist tactics, bombs, murder, and deception were their regimen. All trainees were exposed to physical fitness programs and continual Islamic fundamentalism and militancy. So there was actually a hierarchy of terrorists: the basic "foot soldier"—who was expendable; the skilled guerilla fighter; the lead terrorist for specific missions; the suicide terrorist—who was a "specialist" in bombs and a martyr; and finally, the leaders and organizers of cells and the terrorist network. There were estimated to have been as many as 20,000 trained in the Afghan camps over a five year period, including Taliban fighters. This was a remarkable and frightening accomplishment for a secret organization with no nation.

Al Qaeda developed into a worldwide network of loosely connected terrorist groups in over 50 countries. Such a pervasive danger could not be ignored. To formalize the network, in 1998 bin Laden established the International Islamic Front for Jihad Against Jews and Crusaders. This was a global alliance with Islamic terrorist groups from Egypt, Algeria, Pakistan and Bangladesh. The core group of al Qaeda leaders and operatives were only a few hundred, but the extended community of allied organizations comprised thousands. It was said that "even if al Qaeda disappears, the network of terrorists survive".

## THE PROLIFERATION

There were a wide variety of Islamic terrorist groups that shared in anti-Americanism and violence as a weapon. Some were loosely organized networks, others were basically rebel armies. Collectively, they had at their disposal a very large number of terrorists with resources to fight a guerrilla war on many fronts. Many Islamic terrorist groups were in regions outside the Middle East with different local agendas, but shared values and anti-Americanism, such as the Armed Islamic Group in Algeria, Islamic Unity (al Ittihad al Islamiya) in Somalia, the Islamic Defenders Front and Laskar Jihad in Indonesia, the National Islamic Front in Sudan, and the Islamic Movement of Uzbekistan. As a result, these established Islamic extremist groups became a source of terrorists that could be engaged in schemes and attacks on America. They could be drawn from many countries. Afghanistan, Egypt and Palestine were, of course, major sources of terrorists with closely aligned objectives. There were also Terrorist States, such as Iraq and Libya in particular, that provided training bases, weapons, support, and intelligence to fight America. Libyan terrorists shook the world when they bombed Pan Am flight 103 in 1988 resulting in the deaths of 270 innocent passengers and crew. Some other countries had become "spawning grounds" for terrorists, without the overt support of their governments including Syria,

Algeria, Yemen, Pakistan and Saudi Arabia—the "capital" of fundamentalist Islam. Remember that 15 of the 19 hijackers on 911 were Saudis.

The chain of nations in southern Asia that ranged from Singapore, Malaysia, Indonesia and the Philippines was home for a number of militant Islamic groups. Indonesia was considered an "unstable nation of more than 220 million Muslims". Laskar Jihad was a radical Muslim organization founded in Java in 2000 to wipe out Christians, and establish an Islamic state in Indonesia. Their Commander, Jaffar Umar Thalib had fought with the Afghan Mujahadeen, and returned to Indonesia to establish paramilitary training camps and "Koranic schools". Thousands of young men were indoctrinated in radical Islam who later joined local militant groups like the "Hezbollah Front". Malaysia did not require visas for citizens of Islamic countries, so many terrorists were able to move freely in the region. There was also a regional terrorist network that operated in Singapore, Malaysia and the Philippines—Jemaah Islamiyah, the "Islamic Group"—founded in 1993 that targeted Americans and American installations, and the facilities of American companies. These "sleeper cells" and their plans were supported by al Qaeda until they were discovered. The Philippines also had their own home-grown Islamic terrorist organizations in al Harakatul al Islamiyah rebel group, which was also known as Abu Sayyaf, and the larger Moro Islamic Liberation Front—basically a local guerrilla army.

Major terrorist cells were also found in Europe; in Germany and France in particular. The 911 attacks were masterminded and led by the "Hamburg Cell" of al Qaeda including three of the hijackers. There was also a radical Islamic group called the "Caliphate" in Cologne, Germany. It was a group of Turks led by Metin Kaplan (so it was also called the "Kaplan Group") opposed to the secular government in Turkey. A plot was uncovered in 1998 where they had planned to fly an airplane packed with explosives into the mausoleum of Ataturk, the founder of modern Turkey. There was also a potentially large source of terrorists and sympathizers in England. London, in particular, became the "capital of the Arab world". London was filled with Arab "dissident groups" fleeing from Beirut during the civil war in Lebanon, and from "repression" in Egypt and Saudi Arabia. It served as a financial center and refuge for Muslims who numbered more than 2 million in the UK. Terrorists were recruited from England's growing Muslim community. Al Muhajiroun was a militant Islamic political organization headquartered in London with offices in 21 countries to "establish a worldwide caliphate". Spain was the home of the "Soldiers of Allah" and a key al Qaeda cell. Funds were raised for al Qaeda through credit card fraud. In Greece, the "17 November" group waged domestic and anti-American terrorism undeterred from 1973 until their leaders were captured in 2002. France, of course, had to deal with Algerian terrorists from the Armed Islamic Group (GIA) for years. They were responsible for the 1994 hijacking of an Air France jet that resulted in the deaths of seven hostages and the series of bombings in Paris that killed scores, and injured hundreds in the mid-90's. Italy had terrorists from Morocco and Algeria. Egyptian and Tunisian terrorists organized in Belgium. Europe became a sanctuary for militant Islamic cells, attracting terrorists from all over the Arab world.

Central Asia was also another region with large numbers of militant Muslims. This was the ancient "silk road" path to the "Orient". It had many Islamic states; the so-called "stans". There were 55 million people in the former Soviet Union countries of Kazakhstan, Kyrgyzstan, Tajikistan, Uzbekistan, and Turkmenistan. Russia also still had Chechnya, a rebellious Islamic state. Of course, there was Pakistan and Afghanistan, together with populations of more than 150 million. And the western province of China, Xinjiang, was populated with 9 million Chinese Muslims—the Uighurs. This Turkic speaking minority sought a separate Islamic homeland. Their terrorists were trained by al Qaeda in Afghanistan. This was part of what was referred to as "Turkistan", which was a vision of uniting Uzbekistan with the Islamic region of western China. Islamic groups operated in Central Asia to overthrow governments and establish "strict Islamic states". Corruption and poverty were rampant in this region, which became a spawning ground for Islamic militants and eventually al Qaeda members. Although these Islamic states and people shared many common views, they had their own regional and ethnic interests and priorities. The Northern Alliance, which fought the Taliban in Afghanistan, was predominantly led by ethnic Uzbeks and Tajiks with Russian support. Internally, Russia and China cracked down on Islamic militants and rebels. In the case of Russia, they used military force and occupation. In China, there were police actions, including executions. The Islamic Movement of Uzbekistan helped destabilize three nations of the former Soviet Union with the support of bin Laden. Juma Namangani ran a terrorist camp in Afghanistan as part of al Qaeda. The Hizb-ut-Tahir was an Islamic movement to establish "the Caliphate" or religious rule. Afghanistan was particularly attractive for would-be terrorists. It was known to have "3000 km of open borders" with the Taliban terrorist sympathizers in power at the time. Afghanistan actively recruited terrorists for the jihad and became the "international center of Islamic militancy".

Iran had a 500 mile border with the western region of Afghanistan that had a long history of smuggling, drug and arms trade. The Iranian influence in Herat returned after the war to support the Shiite minority, including rearming them with military weapons. This contributed to the destabilization of Afghanistan. Another source of terrorism and instability in the region has been the relationship between Pakistan and India, particularly with respect to the disputed territory of Kashmir. There are several terrorist groups that operate in that region: Harkat-ul-Mujahadeen, Jaish-e-Muhammad, (Army of Muhammad), and

Lashkar-e-Taiba (Army of the Pure), that were both anti-India and America. The militants and terrorists in Kashmir included and were agitated by outsiders; foreigners from the Afghan-Soviet war. The Pakistani terrorist organizations formed a coalition, Lashkar-e-Omar, that was built on their common hatred of the west and training in Afghanistan.

In addition, there were active cells in the USA and Canada as well. Islamic militants operated openly in the United States, hiding under the protection of "religion". These groups individually may not have been a major threat, but as a collective resource, they were a truly terrifying force to deal with. There were also "sleeper cells" in both the USA and Europe that lay hidden from the view of the authorities so that they could plan and execute their attacks in secret for the greatest surprise. "Jamaat ul Fuqra" was an illusive and "obscure" militant Muslim organization of communal groups located in rural areas of the USA that operated for years undetected.

Terrorists from these sources represented a generation of hate and rage. They were born of poverty, subjugation, ignorance, isolation and religious fanaticism. They had no value for life or respect for others— the "non-believers". Most had no knowledge of the real world. Even if they were educated, many of the Islamic fundamentalists were living in the 14$^{th}$ century, when Muslims ruled much of the civilized world. Many were still driven by an ancient Islamic ruling or "fatwa" that called for all out war against "pagan invaders". This was even to be applied if it resulted in the death of innocent Muslims since "they would go to heaven anyway"! Over the years, such political rulings and interpretations became Islamic dogma that was widely accepted as equivalent to the religious doctrine in the writings of the Koran. Many feel that the driving force of Islamic terrorism was the shame and humiliation of losing the once great Islamic Empire of the past. Islam was the driving force behind an economic, military and cultural power that dominated Europe, Africa, India and China between $9^{th}$ to $14^{th}$ centuries. The Islamic Empire began to lose power in $15^{th}$ century, and eventually Islamic nations were colonized and the Ottoman Empire was broken up after the First World War. Many militant Muslims blame the *others* for the decline of Islam, as it was surpassed by both the developed countries in the west, and later, Asia.

———

So how did so many people become terrorists? What was the basic source for thousands of individuals willing to die for a militant Islamic cause? These were primarily young men, typically unemployed, poor and uneducated. They were brought up under tyrannical, oppressive and corrupt governments, and exposed to both fundamentalist and extremist Islam. In Pakistan the Pashtun educated millions of Pakistanis and Afghan boys in fundamentalist Islam, hatred of the West and anti-Americanism. These young boys were prime candidates for militant and terrorist recruits. There was an entirely new generation of potential terrorists and enemies to follow those already in combat. In Palestine, the limitless source of suicide bombers was created out of "cultural despair and desperation", basically, an environment of no hope. High unemployment and poverty contributed to discontent and religious extremism. But in most cases, it was "bad government" that caused the radicalism and fanaticism that led to terrorism. Many Muslim countries lacked the most basic freedoms and opportunities for their people. And when Muslims migrated to western countries they found themselves alienated by their culture.

Out of the *1.6 billion* Muslims worldwide, *one billion* lived in poverty and despair. That was fertile ground to breed terrorists. Just consider the numbers. If you assume, for example, that only around 20% of the impoverished Muslim population were men of an age and position that could make them potential candidates for militancy—that would be around 200 million. What if only one percent of them were indoctrinated as Islamic fanatics? That would be 2 million potential terrorists. If that seems unreasonable, would you believe 0.1%—or more than 200,000 "crazies" to deal with? No matter what the real number is; it is very large. And the names of all these different terrorist organizations may get tiring after a while, but the point is that there are a lot of militant and fanatical Islamic groups all over the world. The US had over 50 known terrorist organizations to watch. There were just too many organizations and individuals to keep track of.

Although most of the terrorist "troops" were uneducated, impoverished and indoctrinated Islamic militants, the leaders, including suicide team leaders, were often educated and from financially well off families. They were radicalized by the corrupt and tyrannical rule of their homeland, and nurtured with hate for America. Osama bin Laden came from one of the elite royal families of Saudi Arabia. Muhammad Atta, the leader of the Hamburg cell and operational commander of the 911 attacks, was a qualified architect and technically respected graduate student.

It obviously took a lot of money to support such a large network of terrorist organizations. In addition to weapons, they needed training, food, lodging and transportation. For major conflicts and sophisticated terrorist operations, there were certainly other expenses. So how were the terrorists financed? Some organizations like Hamas received money from both Islamic charities and private wealth, in addition to sympathetic countries such as Iran. There was a significant source of individual contributors throughout the Middle East including Saudi Arabia and other Gulf states with oil money. Hamas was supported for its charitable works with schools, mosques, orphanages, clinics and libraries, as well as its support to the families of suicide bombers. This support often came from Muslim charities including some in the West, even the

USA, such as the "Holy Land Foundation". Al Qaeda had financial support from legitimate businesses that were controlled by them or their sympathizers. This "terrorist enterprise" included honey, commercial shipping and even a popular jewel stone called Tanzanite. Of course, they also had illegal sources of money from relations with crime syndicates in countries like Spain and India. Even modest funding could support a major terrorist attack. Although they often took a lot of time planning and preparing, there was usually not a significant cash investment required. The 911 attacks were estimated to cost a total of less than $500,000 to support the efforts of the entire terrorist team over a period of several years.

There were a number of countries that were known to harbor terrorists in addition to Afghanistan. Somalia had its own resident Islamic group, and it was where 18 US soldiers were killed in an ambush in Mogadishu in 1993. Some countries like Somalia were "tailor-made" for terrorists. They had no central government. The people were ruled by tribal fiefdoms and warlords. They were impoverished and Muslim. Yemen was bin Laden's homeland and the home of many former Mujahadeen and al Qaeda sympathizers. It was also where the USS Cole was attacked in 2000. Sudan had its National Islamic Front and previous involvement with al Qaeda. It was the target of a US cruise missile attack in 1998. The Philippines had the Abu Sayyaf group and al Qaeda connections. These terrorists often kidnapped foreigners, including Americans, and held them hostage for ransom. And then there was Pakistan. It had an open border with southern Afghanistan that was basically a lawless region controlled by Pashtun tribes. Pakistan also had its own territorial terrorists in the Kashmir jihadis. Of course, some countries actually adopted and supported terrorism as a state sponsored operation. Renegade nations like Iraq, Iran and Libya had been overt threats to the civilized world for years. Others, such as Syria,

North Korea and Cuba reduced their terrorist activity, but would always have to be watched.

## TERRORISM IS NOT NEW

Unfortunately, history if full of examples of religion being used for violence, political and racial ends. The conflicts between Islam and Christendom have gone on for 1400 years! A historical landmark for those that dream of the great Islamic Empire was when Saladin recaptured Jerusalem from the Crusaders in the 12$^{th}$ century. But violence in the name of religion is not uniquely an Islamic phenomenon. Christianity fought terrible religious wars in the 16$^{th}$ & 17$^{th}$ centuries. The USA finally realized that the problem—or enemy—was not Islam or the Arabs, but rather terrorists, violent extremists and anti-Americanism. After all, terrorism and suicide missions have not been limited to Muslims. Japan had its Kamikaze pilots and more recently both the "Red Army" and the Aum Shinrikyo religious cult. Ireland had the Irish Republican Army. And there were also a variety of radical groups in France, Germany and the USA. Terrorism had become a way of life in some parts of the world. America would have to learn from Israel (Jerusalem) and Ireland (Belfast) that lived with it for decades.

The United States had not been immune to terrorism. It had a long history of its own domestic problem that took several forms. There were the racial hate groups, the anti-establishment socialist groups, the anarchists, and even special interest groups, all with extremist views and a record of violent tactics. Domestic terrorism was a real and continuing threat. The bombing of the Murrah Federal Building in Oklahoma City in 1995 killed 168 and injured 853. International terrorist organizations, however, were a larger threat and doing more damage. Fanatics, in general, were inherently "evil". They were often ruthless, and responsible for atrocities. And the "rules" of war with terrorism were not fair. Terrorists can afford failures as long as they have occasional successes; at least one major "victory". But the targeted enemy of terrorists cannot afford any failures. 911 was a dramatic example of how great the cost of failure could be. Many civilized people eventually came to believe that "you can't deal with crazies"—you can only eliminate them.

# THE EARLY YEARS

## THE SLEEPING GIANT: The initial response

When Japan bombed Pearl Harbor in 1941, the Commander-in-Chief of the Japanese Combined Fleet, Admiral Yamamoto, made a memorable remark that he feared they had "awakened a sleeping giant and have instilled in him a terrible resolve". The American response to that unprecedented attack was massive and fierce. To end the war took almost cataclysmic measures; massive fire bombing of Tokyo, followed by the first and only use of nuclear weapons. America rallied behind the war cry of "Remember Pearl Harbor". In the case of 911, the country recovered quickly from the shock and began to organize a broad-based early reaction and response. "Remember the Towers" became the new rallying cry. While dealing with the trauma and destruction from the attacks, actions were initiated at the federal, state and local levels to deal with the continued threat. This took three basic forms: initial security actions to provide immediate protection of the population from further terrorist attacks; a worldwide search for the terrorists responsible for the horrible events; and the bombing and infiltration of Afghanistan, which was believed to be harboring al Qaeda leadership. The early US campaign, called "Enduring Freedom" was designed to be comprehensive and aggressive, but it was known even then that it might take a long time to accomplish the goals. Much has been written about the initial response of the US to the 911 attacks, but these early years were only the beginning of the war against terrorism, and the events that ultimately would change the world.

The initial security actions in the United States were widespread and very visible. Travel, especially by air, became an unpleasant experience with the increased burden of rigorous screening procedures. Commercial airliners improved security on board with Air Marshalls, secure cockpits and stun guns for pilots. Major public events became high security military exercises, such as the World Series, the Super Bowl and the Olympics. Site preparation, armed guards, screenings, video surveillance and even flyovers became routine, with the US Secret Service assigned to coordinate security. The traditional climate of freedom of movement in the USA had changed dramatically. But the limitations and shortcomings of security systems became visible, even after the crackdown. The security of air travel, for example, was still highly dependent on the check-in procedures. Airport security was conducted by relatively low skilled, minimum wage workers who were employed and managed by the lowest bidder contractors. Major lapses in security continued to occur, so the government decided that it would have to control airport security.

While trying to establish a safe environment at home, efforts were initiated to hunt down and destroy the terrorist networks and leadership. The search began for "terrorist groups of global reach"—a worldwide dragnet. The Foreign Terrorist Tracking Force coordinated federal efforts to keep terrorists out of the US, as well as hunt them down. Everything was suspect: accidents, threats and suspicious looking people. There were extensive worldwide investigations resulting in over 1000 arrests and detentions in the USA alone within the first few months. And hundreds of other suspects were arrested in other countries as well. Financial actions were taken against the terrorists to freeze assets and dry up their sources of funding. In total, $80 billion in assets of 170 organizations and individuals were frozen that had been linked to supporting the Taliban and al Qaeda. Islamic charities and foundations were identified that acted as fronts for funneling money to terrorist groups. But the network was too large and diverse, including the vast "chain" of moneychangers throughout the Muslim world. The United States appealed to all nations in the UN for support in the war on terrorism including intelligence, financial action and military logistics. It was felt that the "future of civilization [was] threatened" by terrorists with weapons of mass destruction.

The rapid and comprehensive deployment and implementation of both security and investigative actions was remarkable. Never had there been such a well-coordinated response at all levels of government, and involving all of its agencies throughout the entire country. However, the constant atmosphere of a high level of alert raised anxiety throughout the country, and often resulted in confusion, fear and anger. There were many incidents of over-reaction; mistaken arrests, detentions and false warnings of additional terrorist attacks. Every potential risk was viewed with suspicion. The reactions of some people approached paranoia; acquiring gas masks, biohazard shelters and radiation detectors. Law enforcement agencies were overwhelmed with false leads and hoaxes. Some were found to be deliberate attempts by terrorist groups to divert attention from their real plans. It was impossible to sort out which were true threats. The government faced a major challenge in dealing with the public's anxiety, while trying to avoid panic.

The United States began building a coalition against terrorism with a number of other countries around the world, including some unlikely partners like Pakistan and Russia. And, of course, America initiated a major air and ground war in Afghanistan to overthrow the Taliban and root out al Qaeda terrorists. The campaign was referred to as a "fight for American values"—to "defend our way of life". The initial phase of the war moved quickly as the Taliban and al Qaeda fighters were driven from cities and towns by heavy US air attacks, with limited support from the Alliance forces on the ground. This was followed by a rapid ground war by Alliance forces with US air and Special Forces support, together with other allies. Foreign soldiers, mostly Pakistanis and Arabs, fought with and led the Taliban during these conflicts. But early "victories" by the allied forces did not include capturing the Qaeda leadership. They were holed up in massive and deep cave complexes for months until many of them were able to escape. It was much more difficult and costly to track down the remaining enemy in the mountainous regions of Afghanistan. The Tora Bora region had a complex of more than thirty caves, some greater than 1000 feet deep. And the Shaikot area of eastern Afghanistan had high mountains at altitudes between 8 to 12,000 feet with a network of old smuggling trails that led east to Pakistan. The American forces eventually had to take the lead in fighting this phase of the war.

The war in Afghanistan was only the first step. America was forced to branch out in order to track down and break the terrorist network. The border areas of Afghanistan and its neighboring countries provided refuge for many of the Taliban and al Qaeda forces. It was relatively easy for them to blend into the lawless regions of Pakistan, Iran and Uzbekistan. The job of hunting down the leadership, and preventing them from regrouping their forces would be long and difficult without local support. In the meantime, the US initiated efforts in other terrorist hotbeds. They exerted political and military pressure on Iraq and Iran, while increasing intelligence activities. American forces also provided assistance to the Philippines to root out the Abu Sayyaf guerrillas in the southern region of the country. This was all a slow and expensive process that provided time for the terrorist networks to recover after the war in Afghanistan. US military advisors were also sent to Somalia, Yemen and Georgia to hunt for terrorists, but these traditional safe harbors were not really committed to cleaning up their acts. These were not countries friendly to America.

Although Pakistan was an important US ally during the Afghanistan war, it had its own problems. Many of the Taliban and al Qaeda were Pakistanis. Some escaped the war in Afghanistan and returned home to rejoin other Islamic militants in Pakistan. They were disillusioned after defeat in Afghanistan, and began a series of terrorist attacks within Pakistan: bombings, kidnappings, killings and assassinations. These were often attacks on foreigners. This internal turmoil only added to the continued instability caused by the conflicts with India over the Kashmir region. Life in Karachi was like living in an armed camp. Pakistan was neither a safe nor reliable country.

The kidnapping and murder of Daniel Pearl, the bureau chief for the Wall Street Journal, was an early clue as to how dangerous and pervasive the network of terrorists actually was. This was not a random act by an isolated group of militants in Pakistan to protest the captivity of their comrades in Guantanamo Bay. It was a link in a series of events over a period of years that could have been prevented. Ahmed Omar Sheikh was arrested and convicted as the ringleader of the kidnapping group. He was a member of the Army of Muhammad that had been founded in Pakistan in 2000. It turned out that the Pakistani Intelligence Service— the "Inter-Services Intelligence"/I.S.I.—had provided liaison and support to this, and other terrorist organizations, including the Taliban, which opposed India's presence in Kashmir. This "evil circle" fostered terrorism in the region. Sheikh had previously been involved in the kidnapping of tourists in India in 1994. He was captured and jailed at the time, only to be freed when an India Airlines plane was hijacked in 1999. Tragically, he was left to live freely in Pakistan, where he organized the kidnapping and horrific execution of Pearl. A sad lesson about the price of negotiating with terrorists!

The initial responses to the 911 attacks focused on the immediate enemy and the known concentrations of organized terrorist groups. Although the haven in Afghanistan that served and nurtured the global terrorist network for a decade had been destroyed, there were still numerous safe harbors for them to regroup and rebuild. Despite the "victories" of conventional warfare, there was nothing done to prevent further internal conflicts and guerrilla wars that followed in this troubled region. America, at first, felt committed to rebuild and stabilize Afghanistan, but it finally abandoned all hope when it was betrayed by the return to corruption, lawlessness and internal terrorism. The tactical war in Afghanistan was inadequate to weed out all of the terrorists, who were spread throughout the world. It only disabled the infrastructure and support system in one country. This was just the first phase of what would prove to be a long and difficult war on terrorism.

## THE INTELLIGENCE FAILURES

While the United States was aggressively pursuing the enemy, there was a growing concern about how all of this could have happened without detection. It was soon concluded that 911 was a major failure of US Intelligence. The terrorist team operated undetected for over a year in the US with frequent travel in and out of the country. The team leader was in the US on an expired visa. There had been alerts and leads, but inadequate follow through. These terrorists were taught unobtrusive techniques in their appearance, actions and communications. Even though some of the 911 terrorists were on the CIA's "watch list", they did not draw the attention of Authorities. The terrorists operated openly without detection. They applied for student visas to attend flight school. One of the planned hijackers was actually held in captivity prior to 911 because of his suspicious actions during flight training. But this did not reveal the plot. They had valid driver's licenses. They even charged airline tickets to their credit cards—all using their own real names! These guys were not even trying to hide their actions. And despite the prior attacks and foiled plots, including the previous bombing of the World Trade Center, this complex plan of terror proceeded almost without any problems. This was a wake up call for both the US Intelligence and law enforcement communities; a lesson learned in the most tragic of hard ways.

It took a post mortem investigation of the specific details to reveal the extent of the problems that had to be fixed. Unfortunately, this also raised the painful question of why this tragedy could not have been prevented. The warning signs were there, and growing for several years. One of the 1995 terrorist team that plotted to hijack 12 US airliners over the Pacific confessed to a plan for crashing airliners into US government buildings—including the Pentagon. In 1999 an intelligence scenario was developed by the Federal Research Division of the Library of Congress for the National Intelligence Council, which was part of the CIA. The report was entitled "The Sociology and Psychology of Terrorism: Who Becomes a Terrorist and Why?" It cited al Qaeda specifically as the "new generation of Islamic terrorists" and claimed that "al Qaeda poses the most serious terrorist threat to US security interests". And it predicted an increased threat of international terrorism with more destruction, including attacks on the USA in particular. Some of the specific excerpts from the report were very disturbing, and should have received more attention:

- "Suicide bombers belonging to al Qaeda's Martyrdom Battalion could crash-land an aircraft packed with high explosives into the Pentagon, the headquarters of the CIA or the White House."
- "Ramzi Yousef had planned to do this against the CIA."
- "Whatever form an attack may take, bin Laden will most likely retaliate in a spectacular way for the cruise missile attack against his Afghan camp in August 1998."

During the year prior to 911 there was increasing evidence of al Qaeda preparations for some kind of airplane terrorism. It turned out that six of the 911 hijackers were trained at US flight schools. Of course, with around 2000 flight schools in US and 20,000 students you might expect that they would be difficult to detect. However, there were multiple clues and warnings. During the trial for the embassy bombings there was testimony that revealed a number of examples of al Qaeda operatives training to be pilots. In February 2001, a flight school in Phoenix alerted the FBI to a suspicious Arab student who later turned out to be one of the hijackers of the plane that crashed into the Pentagon. Later in July, a FBI agent in Phoenix sent a warning to FBI Headquarters about al Qaeda sending students to flight schools to train terrorist pilots. In August 2001, the President was briefed on the potential for al Qaeda hijacking airliners. Around the same time Zacarias Moussaoui, the so-called "20th hijacker", was arrested after raising suspicions at a flight training school. Months earlier the CIA knew of a 911 hijacker and his connection to the Cole bombing, but did not inform other agencies— the FBI and State Department in particular. His visa was renewed, so he could re-enter the US and be part of the infamous team. It turned out to be a little too late when the CIA warned that two suspects from the bombing of the Cole may have entered the USA— men who later turned out to be part of the team that crashed the plane into the Pentagon. During this period, Egyptian Intelligence warned the US of an imminent attack prior to 911 based on infiltrating al Qaeda. There was even a report that the Son of Sheik Omar Abdel Rahman, Assad Allah Abdul Rahman, met with Osama bin Laden to seek help with plans to free his father, which included the use of hijacking airliners.

The agencies just did not connect all the pieces, and they missed opportunities. The FBI was organized and staffed to catch bank robbers and kidnappers. It was not adequately prepared to prevent terrorism. The FBI even captured and released one of original members of the team that bombed the World Trade Center in 1993, who then escaped to Iraq for safe haven. And the INS released wanted aliens because it didn't have the resources to handle them. Despite the repeated incidents and clues, the FBI, CIA and INS did not communicate, so no one saw the whole picture. As a result of these revelations months later, there was a lot of talk throughout the nation about "woulda, coulda, shoulda"—but it was too late for the victims of 911. The media and politicians focused on second-guessing and criticizing the oversights and faults of the government agencies, distracting them from the job at hand, which was to increase the pressure on terrorists. The agencies spent time answering the questions of Congress and the media, and also engaged in trying to cover their tracks and finger point, when they needed to concentrate on preventing the next attack! Now just suppose the President was told in August of 2001 that al Qaeda planned an attack on the US in the near future based on reliable sources—perhaps involving an airplane hijacking. What would/should/could he have done?? It was time for the US to look forward and move on.

## THE CREEPING COMPLACENCY

Within a few months the war was no longer "front page" or affecting everyone's life. Things seemed to be back to normal, but the threats were still there—and real. Only the military and security forces were fighting the war. The tributes seemed to become "routine". Opening ceremonies, color guards, anthems, flags—all meant to be patriotic and supportive, but beginning to get a little "old". It had all been done before. Many felt that it was time to move on as America had so many times before after previous tragedies and wars. Even the brave firefighters got tired and depressed from attending the seemingly endless funerals and memorials. All of the flags and signs began to disappear. People began to ask how long we need to fight this war on terrorism. When will all the bombing and arrests be enough?

There began to develop a sense of disillusionment within the USA. Questions were being asked at all levels:
- Why no quick end to the terrorist network?
- Why can't we capture Osama bin Laden?
- Why is it so difficult to fight in some impoverished country that is still living in the Stone Age?
- Why is it taking so long?
- How many more lives must we lose to terrorism?

At the same time, there was growing dissatisfaction with the mismanagement and corruption involved with the settlements and charitable funds for the 911 victims and rescue workers. Law suits and insurance settlement cases were tied up for years delaying and jeopardizing relief for victim's families and businesses. The government's Victims Compensation Fund was plagued by bureaucratic and legal delays. It was established by Congress to assist the families of victims as well as rescue workers at a cost of approximately $6 billion. That was just too much money to be administered fairly and efficiently on an individual basis. The settlement process was complicated. It required adjustments for insurance and other compensation. And it did not apply to others impacted by the 911 attacks, such as local businesses. The Federal Emergency Management Agency/FEMA also provided for relief to families impacted by the attacks by helping with bills in particular, such as mortgage and rental assistance. Although FEMA distributed $65 million, it was only a fraction of what it had done in past disasters. But 911 was not a typical disaster. Even so, FEMA was very restrictive. Thousands of individuals were denied benefits; in fact, 70% of those who applied. In addition to seeming to be unfair, the agency was perceived to be plagued with mismanagement and mistakes.

Charities had also collected an additional $2 billion for relief of the tragedy. When you suddenly dump hundreds of millions of dollars in the hands of an organization, no matter how well intentioned, you can expect problems. There were also delays and mismanagement of these funds; bureaucracy, errors, and even inequities in the distribution of charitable contributions, such as between uniformed workers families and civilian victims. The rules for beneficiaries were narrowly defined. They were to apply only to those directly affected, which left many others without relief that were considered only indirectly affected; again the local businesses. On the other hand, there were those that compared the settlements with those of the Oklahoma City bombing, where only modest expense payments were made, and felt that all this money was inequitable. Then there were the fraudulent claims filed with charities and government agencies, scams to defraud victims out of benefit money and theft of assets from relief agencies. Criminals just have no shame! All of this was unconscionable to most Americans who had laid their hearts out, and, in many cases their contributions, to help those in need.

While the American public became more disenchanted, it also grew tired of the unending high alert status. The repeated warnings continued, but there were no attacks. People began to feel like the government was "crying wolf too often" and some became annoyed. This was aggravated by a rash of over-reactions. The false arrests, unwarranted detentions and harsh treatment of suspects became an embarrassment to the American justice system. There even seemed to be no basis or evidence for the prosecution of the 500 "most dangerous" al Qaeda captives held in Guantanamo. The public began to question whether this was a fair price to pay for security. There was also a growing fear among the people and the politicians of this becoming another Vietnam. They were reminded that the Soviet Union was bogged down in the quagmire of an Afghan war for more than a decade before they finally withdrew in defeat. The war was dragging on and the enemy was still at large. Innocent civilians were being killed and injured in the massive bombing campaigns as well as with incidents of misdirected targets. And then there were the friendly fire incidents that killed and injured Allied and US forces. Most of those old enough to remember Vietnam did not want to go through this again. American politicians and the public began to be more interested in the poor economy—jobs, deficits, and the stock market—than in the war on terrorism. Most parts of the country lost interest in the war on terrorism. It became old news—"all Osama all the time", and the war had not come to their town or region. People just wanted to "move on" and get on with their lives. They were tired of seeing the ads from every major company and country on why *they* were so sorry about the World Trade Center—and spending a lot of money to tell you!

As time passed without incident in the USA, some of the high security measures instituted after 911 were relaxed. The costs of maintaining special air surveillance, extra local police patrols, and federal security coverage at major public events and transportation centers became too much of a burden. State and local governments could not afford to continue at this level. They had other problems to address, especially in a weak economy. At the federal level, the Administration still had a foreign war to fight while it tried to stimulate the economy. Domestic security was getting too expensive. American politics started to drift back to business as usual. The President no longer had free reign to implement policy without a dogfight with Congress. And the politicians began to focus on their own constituencies and re-election priorities. America relaxed its guard.

In the meantime, America's "allies" lost interest in continuing the war. They felt it was time to "stop beating a dead horse". Enough is enough. They did not share America's commitment to continue the campaign beyond the initial phase. And the Islamic states in particular, wanted to re-focus on resolving the Israeli-Palestinian conflict as well as their own domestic troubles. The world news became dominated by the escalating war in the Palestinian territories. Terrorism returned to being "Israel's problem". There was pressure on America to return to normalcy and reduce the tension.

The complacency was initially reinforced by the early "victories" of American and anti-Taliban forces; killing and capturing many Taliban and al Qaeda fighters, and regaining control of Afghanistan. The apprehension of al Qaeda operatives, the freezing of their assets and the discovery of evidence that thwarted new terrorist plots gave false hope that the network had been shattered. America forgot that there were tens of thousands of trained terrorists still focused on their militant cause in over 50 countries. So this period of complacency ended traumatically— with new shocks of the terrorist reality.

# THE REIGN OF TERROR—The secondary attacks

The law enforcement community knew that more attacks were inevitable, but there were no clues as to where, when and how. It wasn't long before the terror returned. What started as a few isolated incidents of bioterrorism and failed bombings began a long series of persistent attacks to reinforce the fears in all Americans. These secondary terrorist attacks evolved into what became known as the "Reign of Terror"! America's complacency was short lived, and for years no one felt safe.

Although America tried to prepare for the inevitable follow-up to the 911 attacks, it was just not ready to deal with all the possibilities. The nation was exposed to most of the basic risks with little defense available. America had spent a century developing a very powerful military force and an efficient state of readiness for conventional wars, but not for terrorism. It learned the hard way that it had to always be vigilant. The USA had not lived in the type of environment experienced for decades by Israel, Northern Ireland or Spain. But it also learned that it was facing something more organized, with greater impact, which was inherently evil. The primary objective of terrorists is to create fear and chaos, not necessarily destruction. So they had many possibilities from which to choose. They did not have to be very innovative. They could just watch the media for new ideas and potential sources for their terror!

At first the US realized that 911 brought out "all the crazies". Some were individuals trying to be part of the "Jihad" or jihad warrior "wannabes", including some lone suicide bombers. There was also a wide variety of incidents of localized terrorism and hoaxes, particularly with the mail. After the terrorist attacks of 911, a crime wave began in America. As law enforcement focused on terrorism, it was diverted from covering and protecting against normal crime. These "crimes of opportunity" reversed the previous trend of improvement that the US had been experiencing. While it was waiting for the next round of attacks from the enemy, America soon realized that it needed to strengthen its security for internal risks as well. It wasn't prepared for domestic turmoil, especially after the widespread patriotic response and support for public safety measures. America forgot for the moment that there was still a criminal element in its population to be dealt with that had no qualms about taking advantage of this time of national emergency. This problem ultimately led to a major reprioritization in government funding of security at all levels, and resulted in an across the board crackdown on all types of crime.

The Reign of Terror was triggered by the fall of the Taliban and al Qaeda forces in Afghanistan. It took time for the international terrorist networks to regroup and organize their plans. The terrorist groups were disrupted by the US war on terrorism. Their sources of funding were cut off. They lost many of their leaders in the Afghan war. Their training camps, safe houses and underground fortresses were destroyed. Key members of terrorist cells were arrested in many countries. Initially, this led to a series of unsophisticated and low cost attacks by individuals and small groups, until the terrorist networks could get organized again. America was not ready for the secondary attacks. In particular, the

Heartland of America that really didn't directly experience the trauma of 911 thought that "it would never happen here!" But then, al Qaeda awakened their "sleeper cells".

## BIOLOGICAL & CHEMICAL TERRORISM

The first threat to be exposed was bioterrorism. Although there was military research for decades, the American public did not understand the potential scope and magnitude that was involved. Chemical and biological weapons can take many forms; some limited in their impact, others deadly and widespread. The biological agents are bacteria or viruses used for "germ warfare". Anthrax spores could be deadly if inhaled. Their incubation period varies from two weeks to two months after exposure, making their source hard to trace. If untreated, inhalation anthrax is fatal in 90% of cases. Antibiotics are only effective if used within the first few days. It turned out that there were many sources of weapons grade anthrax, including US military laboratories. There were also hundreds of research laboratories with samples available. In addition, there were 46 germ banks worldwide with anthrax cultures. Many were in locations that were relatively easy to access by international terrorists, such as Teheran in Iran, Istanbul in Turkey, Calcutta in India, Bangkok in Thailand and Sofia in Bulgaria. Many sites were found in Afghanistan— around 40—that had been used to develop biological and other weapons of mass destruction to train and export to their terrorist cells in other countries. There was evidence found that al Qaeda considered dispersing anthrax using balloons, but this was a primitive, inefficient, and very visible approach. Anthrax could be a devastating weapon. A source equivalent to a five pound bag of flour could kill half the population of Washington, DC. The early mail attacks proved how easy it was to deploy anthrax and how widely it could be spread.

Smallpox, on the other hand, was a virus, not bacteria. It was carried by aerosols that were extremely contagious and not effected by antibiotics. Smallpox was more dangerous than anthrax, and had been the biggest medical killer in 20th century. The vast program of past vaccinations had ended in the 1970s after the threat of smallpox was eliminated. But there was no protection after ten years, so almost everyone was vulnerable. Salmonella could also be used as a "bacterial weapon", and some strains were resistant to antibiotics. There was a major food poisoning incident in 1984 when a local cult sprayed it on salad bars. Then there were chemical weapons. This included "nerve gas" such as Sarin, which was first used by the Nazis and more recently by terrorists in Tokyo in 1995. It could even be spread by aerial attack, like from a crop duster. Cyanide gas could be used to kill small numbers of people since it is not easily deployed on a large scale. A common liquid fertilizer, anhydrous ammonia, could be turned into a toxic gas when exposed to air, and Ricin was a very potent poison that could be manufactured from chemicals that were available from many potential commercial sources. Chemical and biological weapons offered a wide variety of options and opportunities for terrorists.

The Soviet Union had a "massive decades-long program" of developing chemical and biological weapons. They worked on anthrax, typhus, plague and tularemia. Large quantities of anthrax spores were stored on an island in Central Asia by Russia in the 1980's: Vozrozhdeniye in Uzbekistan in the Aral Sea. Some Soviet scientists were later recruited by Iran and Iraq in the 1990s to help start their programs. It was also known that Libya, Syria and North Korea had developed bioterrorism weapons. The Soviet weapons factories and dumping grounds became sources of "weapons grade" biological materials that were moved in small quantities from Russia and former Soviet Union states to Iraq, and eventually to the Qaeda network.

The first incidents of bioterrorism were a few envelopes sent in the US Mail containing weapons grade anthrax spores. Although these incidents killed five people and only thirteen others got ill, they were extremely effective in creating an environment of disruption and terror. In addition to the exposure of the recipients, a broader impact was discovered from cross-contamination exposure during mail processing. A couple of letters spread anthrax infections in six states. There were also a series of "copycat" hoaxes. The point was made that no one was safe from terrorists who had access to toxic biological materials. It only took one individual with access to a small quantity of weapons grade anthrax spores to terrorize the US Postal Service and an entire nation. Immediate and comprehensive action had to be taken to restore some level of confidence in the mail. Postal personnel were protected with gloves and masks. Antibiotics were prescribed for 30,000 high risk workers. The physical security of the mail system was improved through screening and machine maintenance, as well as isolation of suspect packages and shipments of mail. There was even selected use of sterilization processes to kill possible germs. But with the billions of pieces of mail that are processed, there was no way to assure its total safety. Incidents of contaminated mail occurred again and again until the system was significantly changed enough to provide adequate prevention and protection.

What America did not realize at the time was that with the unintentional help of the very thorough free press in the USA, terrorists were able to improve the effectiveness of their attacks. In the case of bioterrorism, for example, they learned to remove the static electric charge from anthrax spores to permit them to disperse more easily— a minor, but deadly improvement. The major focus on securing the mail also diverted attention from other exposures. With sources for an array of biological and chemical materials, terrorist groups considered targets and deployments that would be unexpected and relatively easy to execute. An outdoor aerosol release of anthrax could infect thousands who would disperse widely and be difficult to detect in time. Logical targets were public events that attracted large crowds of people in a relatively unprotected environment. The terrorists considered celebrations, holidays, parades and sporting events for the best candidates. New York City, of course, offered the Thanksgiving and Saint Patrick's Day Parades, and the New Years Eve celebration in Times Square, but New York remained on high alert with massive police and security coverage of these events. Everyone and every event was suspect in New York. The Olympics were also attractive for maximum international impact and TV coverage, but extraordinary security measures were taken to protect them. There was also the annual Rose parade in Pasadena. Who would expect terrorism to strike this joyous tradition in southern California? Or one of the many major league football and baseball games held in large stadiums throughout the USA. Some were even held in indoor facilities that could be very effective targets. How could they all be covered adequately?

The enemy was looking for not only an opportunity for success, but a dramatic symbolic act of terror on the "American devil". Why not target a baseball game—the American pastime? But instead, they chose Mardi Gras in New Orleans—a Christian symbol that they looked on as a pagan ritual of the infidels. A lone terrorist was dispatched with a modest supply of weapons grade anthrax to disperse in the large, tightly packed and jubilant crowds of Bourbon Street. In costume like all the others in the parade, he wandered the streets and bars undetected. His costume mask concealed his facemask, and, with the added protection of antibiotics, he went about his deadly task without fear. Disguised as a King, the gentle movements of his scepter delivered lethal doses to hundreds of innocent revelers. It was several weeks after the Mardi Gras tourists had returned to their homes all over the country that the outbreak of inhalation anthrax was detected. The antibiotic Cipro® had

proven to be effective against anthrax infections, and an anthrax vac-
cine was available, but by the time the investigation led to the common
source, it was too late for the victims. How could they know who to protect—where and when? Hundreds died. This time, the terror of public
insecurity hit the nation hard.

The success of this attack encouraged the terrorists. They worked
hard to develop additional targets for their biological and chemical war
chest that could be just as effective. What they were looking for was
something that would be relatively low in cost with a high probability of
succeeding. They considered indoor targets. A relatively small volume
of finely milled anthrax spores could be dispersed throughout an air
handling system to infect all the occupants of a large building. This
could be any one of many major high-density buildings, such as skyscrapers, arenas, indoor stadiums, schools or hotels. It didn't have to be
a landmark; an obvious target that already had high levels of security.
There were still endless possibilities all across the country. New York,
Chicago and Washington, DC were just too risky. But Boston was just
right, and so was San Francisco. There had been active cells in those
areas for years and there were many potential targets. All it took was for
one man to get a job as a janitor or maintenance man at a major office
building in each city. The targets chosen were not the most prominent
skyscrapers, but the government centers with thousands of workers in
federal offices. On one fateful day, a coordinated attack was made on
both facilities. The terrorists released their toxins through the intakes to
the buildings' central air handling systems. One used anthrax, the other,
cyanide gas. In one case all it took was a relatively small bag of finely
milled anthrax spores. In the other, a can of cyanide powder mixed on
site with sulfuric acid. The results were devastating and fatal. Many died
and many more were seriously injured. Office workers everywhere were
stricken with fear and office buildings would never be the same again.

But this was not enough for the terrorists. They knew they could get away with these bio/chemical attacks, so they continued to develop plans for more targets. The cells were loosely connected by communications and funding, but generally were able to act independently once they agreed on a basic strategy. So another cell prepared their plan to contaminate a water supply. Since there are 168,000 public water supplies in the USA, there were plenty of potential targets all over the country. But it wouldn't be that easy. After 911 this was a recognized exposure. Security controls were put in place all across the nation, at least at the major water supplies, including dams, reservoirs and water treatment facilities. There were guards, patrols and barriers; in some cases even flyovers. It was also commonly believed that terrorists "would need a truckload of chemicals" to contaminate a public water supply. But what about the distribution lines, not just the reservoirs? Or major user facilities such as office buildings and manufacturing plants? There were also public wells that served as water supplies for relatively small towns. These targets were vulnerable and could still terrorize thousands of people at a time. So they did it. One cell attacked the distribution lines of the water supply to a major industrial complex in Detroit—the home of the American automobile. Another attacked one of the public wells serving a residential area in Fairfax County, Virginia—a bedroom community for Washington, DC. It didn't take a truckload of cyanide to do the job. Thousands got sick and hundreds died before the source was discovered and cleaned out. No factory or town felt safe anymore.

The terrorists did not stop there. It almost became a contest between cells to see who could gain the most notoriety for surprise and casualties. Public transportation systems were studied as potential targets. Subways in particular were considered attractive because of their ease of access for spreading either biological or chemical weapons, and the difficulty for people to quickly escape from them. Smallpox was considered, but it had to be spread by aerosol from a contagious body. Although there were volunteers, it was decided that the infected suicide candidate might be too weak to carry out the mission. So they went back to the source of anthrax and prepared a package for a delivery system. A batch of spores was loaded into a dispenser that could be activated from inside a back-pack carried by the terrorist. They selected the Washington, DC Metro, both for maximum exposure and to avoid the more unpredictable and higher security of the New York subway system. He entered the Metro at the Roslyn station during the morning rush hour. It only took a five minute ride through the tunnel to the Foggy Bottom station to walk through a crowded car full of unsuspecting passengers and fatally infect dozens. Washington soon became a military zone.

America was then truly terrorized by the recurring incidents of bio-logical and chemical attacks on the public. It wasn't necessary to risk any more of the same kind of missions. There was still a major vulnera-ble target area. A strategy was developed to attack America's food sup-ply. The objective was not only to create an environment of terror among American consumers, but also to raise serious international doubts about the safety of American exports of food. This "agro-terror-ism" involved a series of exposures of the food supply to contamination and poisoning. The targets were modest in size, but broad in scope and location; a herd of livestock, a chicken farm, a fish hatchery, a dairy farm, and a grain elevator. The incidents of foot and mouth disease, mad cow disease, botulism and salmonella resulted in only a relatively few deaths and illnesses, but the impact on the food supply system was massive. Everything was suspect. American consumers were terrified to shop for fresh foods. The demand for American food exports dropped dramatically. Farms, processors and distributors soon became high security operations.

## CYBER TERRORISM

One of America's greatest strengths and, as it turned out also one of its weaknesses, was the vast network of computer systems that ran the economy. There were thousands of major computer complexes that were interconnected and interdependent in their handling of the billions of transactions that occurred throughout all aspects of business every day. It took only a few talented hackers targeting several weak points to create a wave of cyber terrorism that disrupted the systems critical to America's economy and security; supporting the financial sector, communications, energy, transportation and even government operations. Some acquired jobs as software engineers at key installations with internal access to the primary control systems. Others were able to penetrate system firewalls externally. It wasn't difficult to find the weaknesses. The US government even maintains a public website with an updated list of specific "cyber vulnerabilities". Once the terrorists gained access to the targeted systems, all it took was shutting down a couple of websites and infecting a few others with viruses. The result was a series of power blackouts, bank shutdowns, telephone line disruptions, and air traffic emergencies—random chaos. It didn't take long interruptions or major outages to have a significant effect. Confidence in the security of the information infrastructure was destroyed until a massive effort to restore its integrity was completed. In the meantime, the markets and industries these systems served were seriously impacted.

## BACK TO BASICS

While all this "high tech terror" was being executed, the terrorist network did not forget their traditional weapon of choice—the bomb. They had been trained and experienced in truck bombs like those used so successfully in the Middle East, New York and of course, Oklahoma City. There were a wide variety of potential targets considered including public places and facilities, infrastructure, industry, utilities and transportation. Although much had been done to tighten the security at the most obvious targets, there were still many that were vulnerable. Even though airline security was still not perfect, it had improved significantly and was constantly on high alert, so it was no longer a logical target. However, there were relatively few security controls on alternate means of transportation such as trains, buses and ships. Although there were some measures added, such as requiring a positive ID to purchase tickets, there was virtually no physical security in relation to the screening of either passengers or luggage. It was pretty much "business as usual" on these common modes of transportation, and their traffic actually increased after air travel was impacted by the 911 events. So a "sitting duck" target was selected. A member of the Boston cell embarked on an Amtrak train at South Station on a busy Friday evening before a holiday weekend. It was one of the unreserved Northeast Regional trains headed south and loaded with business commuters as well as college students going home. Like most of the other passengers, he had a large suitcase that he stuffed in the overhead rack with all the others. There is no luggage check in on these busy trains. The luggage racks and seating areas were always full at this time and so were the seats; standing room only. One hour later, he got off the train at Providence where he could take a commuter train right back to Boston. No one noticed him in the crowds of passengers, or that he left his suitcase in the overhead rack. As the train left the station, the bomb in it was activated by remote control. It destroyed the rail car it was in and killed 50 people instantly. The train derailed, fires broke out, hundreds were injured and Amtrak was shut down for days. It was easy. Those travelers who switched from the Shuttle flights to Amtrak after 911 were no longer safe. But rail travel would change.

There was a plan developed for a major attack on a commercial shipping target. This was much more ambitious. The authorities already considered the possible exposure of bombing a tanker of liquefied natural gas in port. So security was tightened on these highly explosive targets. But cargo on container ships and their ports also had the potential for substantial impact. There were approximately 600,000 containers that entered seaports in the USA each day on more than 500 ships. The security was limited with little inspection and a low chance of detection. Container ports were usually in the proximity of other facilities critical to the infrastructure such as major oil and gas storage, interstate highways and rail lines. So it wasn't difficult to prepare a cargo container with a large volume of explosives hidden within a shipment on an al Qaeda controlled commercial ship. It sailed from the Middle East. The container was transferred in Europe where it was then shipped on to the USA. When the container ultimately reached the heavily packed and busy container port of Elizabeth, New Jersey, it was detonated remotely causing widespread damage, death, injuries and disruption. Oil and gas distribution lines exploded spreading the flames to storage tanks. These secondary explosions tore through the crowded rail yard destroying hundreds of tanker cars and the track system. The fires could be seen for miles around the harbor. They took days to put out while the adjacent New Jersey Turnpike had to be closed to all public traffic. The ports of America were now part of the battleground and had to be secured.

There was always a fear that Stinger missiles may get into the hands of terrorists. These shoulder mounted anti-aircraft weapons were supplied by the US CIA to the Afghan rebels to fight the Soviet Union in 1986. They proved to be very effective weapons at close range, particularly against Soviet helicopters. Hundreds were never accounted for after that war. The black markets of Afghanistan and Pakistan found anxious buyers. Some were used by the Taliban and al Qaeda, but a few found their way to other countries through the terrorist network. It was 8:30 on a typical weekday morning outside Washington, DC. The white van pulled off the GW Parkway into the parking lot in Lady Bird Johnson Park beside the Potomac River. Like most mornings at this time, there were no other vehicles in the lot. As the morning line up of airliners waited their turn to take off at Reagan National Airport, the rear door of the van opened. It was a straight shot; really not that difficult. The hourly Shuttle flight to New York was full of passengers, as usual, and of course, also full of fuel. As it rose off the runway the missile tore into its underbelly. The explosion was immediate and deafening. The fireball could be seen for miles. One hundred and ten lives were lost in an instant. The ground controllers were in shock. It took a few minutes before anyone could grasp what had happened and react. In the meantime, the van disappeared into the morning rush hour traffic. There would be no more open perimeters around major airports.

There was also always a role for the lone suicide bomber, and there was no shortage of volunteers for martyrdom. This was still the easiest approach to terror. Suicide bombers became the weapon of choice of the Palestinian terrorists against Israel. The bombs were simple. All it took was a low cost mixture of fertilizer and sugar tied to a "crazy" willing to commit suicide for the sake of homicide. Hamas and the Islamic Jihad wanted to put pressure on the US to make Israel give up the Palestinian territories. But this was a "local issue", not the top priority of international terrorists and al Qaeda in particular. However, al Qaeda found it easy to recruit willing suicide bombers from among the many extremist "martyrdom groups" in Palestine. And they could be imported to the US in container ships without detection. Al Qaeda was interested in creating the maximum impact and terror—not in just killing Jews. So they planned coordinated attacks to occur simultaneously in two cities. The targets were indoor arenas where there were high density events that would always be full. One bomber entered

Madison Square Garden in New York and the other at the STAPLES Center in Los Angeles where the Knicks and Lakers were hosting Sunday afternoon basketball games that were being broadcast live on network TV. During the Star Spangled banner in LA, and near the end of the game in New York the bombers approached the playing floor level for maximum exposure. Dozens were killed and there were hundreds of casualties—for millions to see. The entrances to America's arenas would become security clearance centers. The American tradition of "going to a game" would never be an easy or comfortable experience again.

America had learned the hard way, too many times, that a truck bomb could destroy a building. Why not a bridge or some other major part of the infrastructure? A rented truck was loaded with thousands of pounds of high explosives prepared from the traditional mix of commercially available ammonium nitrate fertilizer and diesel fuel. On a normal weekday in the morning rush hour the martyr-to-be drove the truck into New York's Lincoln tunnel and detonated the bomb. The tube was demolished along with hundreds of vehicles and lives. The scene was more horrific than the special effects of a disaster movie. It would be years before it could be rebuilt, but access to tunnels became a security clearance process more like a border crossing. Traffic into and out of New York and other major cities turned into a nightmare.

## NUCLEAR TERRORISM

Ever since 911, one of the greatest fears was a terrorist attack on a nuclear power plant. Some were particularly attractive targets since they were in locations near high-density populations. Indian Point was in the most densely populated area of any nuclear power plant. There were 20 million people within a 50 mile radius. There were many other potential targets—over 100 active nuclear power plants in the USA. The public concern in those areas was so great that some counties even distributed potassium iodide pills as a precaution against thyroid cancer from exposure to nuclear radiation. In addition to the possibility of a bombing causing an uncontrolled nuclear reaction, there was more than 50,000 tons of radioactive nuclear waste stored at these facilities that would also be at risk of a significant release of radiation. The terrorists were very interested in the prospects and spent years in researching the possibilities. They found easy access to detailed documents of the design and layout of plants that were publicly available. Although there were measures taken to heavily protect them, security at nuclear power plants in the United States was known to be inadequate from the poor results they had on NRC drills. In particular, they were not prepared against sophisticated or large scale attacks. Access to a nuclear power plant or its proximity was difficult, except from the air. At first it was thought that there was an exposure to small airplanes, but it was determined that they couldn't penetrate a fuel containment facility with its 12-foot thick walls. It would take a fully fueled, full size jet. This, of course, was not unprecedented, but extremely difficult after 911. Research also revealed that even the Chernobyl disaster did not result in a large number of fatalities, so attacking a nuclear power plant did not offer the terrorists a "high yield potential". Fortunately, the plans were eventually abandoned for easier attacks.

The decision to pass up nuclear power plants did not mean that the terrorists were no longer interested in creating nuclear terror. Nuclear weapons were even more attractive. They could cause the most lethal attack. One nuclear explosion can kill many thousands of people instantly as well as cause massive destruction, and a large number of additional casualties, including long-term radiation exposure that could remain dangerous for many years. The potential impact was much larger than that of the 911 attacks. A one-kiloton nuclear bomb, less than 10% of the size of the Hiroshima bomb, could destroy a one square mile area with potentially hundreds of thousands of casualties. The Qaeda network pursued the acquisition of nuclear materials and weapons for years. Many potentially viable sources were available. There were 50,000 nuclear warheads in the US and Russian arsenals. But these were all protected with complex security codes, well guarded and accounted for. However, the former Soviet Union had stockpiles at a number of old facilities, some of which were now independent countries, including Islamic states. Many of these facilities had poor and questionable security, and were in regions with rampant corruption— all potentially ripe sources for the terrorist network. There were nuclear weapons in rogue states like Iraq, Libya and North Korea, also potentially sympathetic sources for the terrorists. In addition to weapons, there were also available sources of radioactive materials. The spent fuel from nuclear power plants throughout the world was stored in relatively small transportable containers. Of course some of these nuclear power plants were also in the same countries that supported and harbored terrorists. And there were millions of gallons of radioactive waste from nuclear weapons production. Just one cup of this liquid could deliver fatal doses of radiation to a room full of people.

There were also old weapons depots with storage facilities from the cold war. Russia had even developed nuclear bombs in a "suitcase". It was reported that bin Laden had purchased some of these mini-nukes from cooperative Chechens. Since the fall of the Soviet Union, a black market developed in nuclear weapons and materials. There was also access to nuclear materials and intelligence from Pakistani weapons experts, but a nuclear bomb is very complex and sophisticated. They were not simple to maintain, transport or operate. And they would be too difficult for terrorists to build. Even for a relatively small nuclear weapon you need a reasonably large quantity of highly enriched uranium; more than 100 pounds. Although there was more than 1000 tons in the US and Russian stockpiles, it was too difficult to obtain. However, lower grade nuclear materials were much more readily available, such as from spent fuel and medical sources. The enemy found that there were cheaper alternatives to military nuclear weapons. By using conventional bombs to disperse radioactive materials they could kill and sicken large numbers of people as well as contaminate land and buildings. The "dirty bomb" was a more attractive and practical alternative. This approach also opened up a wide variety of potential sources of radioactive materials. The possibilities included more accessible commercial sources, such as radioactive cobalt used in the medical and food industries, as well as nuclear waste from the power and military sectors. The US even discovered that there were hundreds of radioactive devices missing from its defense arsenal. As the terrorists improved their sources and handling of hazardous and radioactive materials, they explored the many options available to them, and prepared their plans.

The real challenge turned out to be the selection of a viable target more so than assembling the weapon. The most obvious targets for such an attack were heavily guarded locations with difficult access. Although a major commercial or military complex would be a very desirable target for a nuclear weapon, they did not offer a high probability of success without a sophisticated and expensive delivery system. The terrorists were always aware that they were not a true military force with access to jet bombers or missiles, but they were very resourceful in finding relatively crude approaches to their attacks that worked. With the help of Iraq and the support of the Qaeda coalition, including Hezbollah, they obtained the nuclear materials and assembled a dirty bomb. It was ultimately concealed in a common delivery truck that was parked in a busy commercial sector of a major population center and then detonated. It was a powerful bomb that caused a lot of fatalities and destruction, and the subsequent radiation exposure was devastating. Tel Aviv became a death camp—and remained uninhabitable for many years.

# HIND SIGHT

The Reign of Terror had reached the epitome of unspeakable horror. No one was safe—anywhere, anytime. Both the mightiest military force in the world and the nation with the tightest security seemed to be impotent against the global terrorist network. How could this Reign of Terror have happened? Why wasn't it prevented by the War on Terrorism?

Hindsight is easy when given the facts of history. It doesn't take any special talent of perception to point out mistakes and omissions after you experience the consequences. But looking back can be productive. It can not only explain why things happened, but more importantly, reveal what can be learned for the future. The War on Terrorism could have been more successful and probably a lot easier. And perhaps the Reign of Terror could have been prevented.

## AMERICA'S ALLIES

The War on Terrorism had fatal flaws from the start. Even the traditional "friends" and "allies" of the USA were not completely behind the effort. The western industrialized countries that shared much of the American cultural heritage were found to have at least some of their population sympathetic with the militant Islamic cause. This seemed to be retribution for the US role in dominating economic, political and military power in the world. There was a failure to build a strong coalition of major western countries to fight terrorism. The support of the allies was modest and short term with little, if any, military involvement. Only the "Coalition Allies", including the UK and Canada, committed forces to active military roles along with the USA. Other European "allies" opposed some of the aggressive US actions and the post Afghan strategy. This uneasiness with the US position was aggravated by unilateral actions, the abandonment of international treaties, and what were perceived as harsh legal actions—such as detentions, trials, and executions. Many countries opposed the death penalty in principle. There was even a conspiracy theory in Europe that the 911 attacks were part of a US government plot to justify wars in Afghanistan and Iraq.

The Rest Of the World (ROW) thought it was "America's Problem". To fight terrorism, Washington made partnerships with countries and leaders with records of tyranny, oppression, and human rights violations, such as Pakistan and Uzbekistan—not the best kinds of allies! America's "new allies" could not be trusted. They were all inherently anti-American. They just happened to also oppose al Qaeda and the Taliban. Even Arabs previously grateful to the USA for fighting the Gulf War, like Kuwait and Saudi Arabia, were opposed to the US military action in Afghanistan.

There were factions within the anti-Taliban Alliance forces. They comprised a variety of ethnic groups including Tajiks, Uzbecks, Hazaras and Pashtuns as well as "tribes" within the groups. The Pashtun were the largest group, comprising almost 40% of the population, and were concentrated in the Southeast region along the border with Pakistan. The Tajiks and Hazaras were next in size and comparable to each other, while the Uzbeks were a relatively small regional minority. Each had their own cultural heritage and geographical domain. There was skepticism and disagreement between and within the tribes in Afghanistan about alignment with the USA. Many were Pashtun like the Taliban and most Pakistanis. Pakistan's northern border with Afghanistan was controlled by Pashtuns who had no interest in or support for America's objectives. Afghanistan was a region of historical ethnic rivalries between the northern and southern tribes; the Pashtun and Pakistanis versus the Uzbecks and Tajiks. Some groups were fundamentalist Muslims and others were moderate. There were also differences in the attitudes and convictions between the older and younger generations of Afghanistan. This was not a unified people fighting a common enemy. The ethnic factions in Afghanistan made both peace and unified military and political coalitions impractical. The US support of the Northern Alliance, comprised primarily of Uzbecks and Tajiks, often put them at odds with the Pashtuns and Pakistanis of the southern region.

The war in Afghanistan had its victories and was relatively swift, but failed to achieve its objectives. Many called for the US to "bomb Afghanistan back into the Stone Age". But what became a cruel joke was that they couldn't—because "Afghanistan was still in the Stone Age"! America chose to depend on its allies to help with the execution of the war. The international coalition played a limited military role, but provided valuable political support to the US presence in Afghanistan. To limit US casualties and reinforce the concept that this was Afghanistan's war, America relied on the Alliance forces in Afghanistan to take the lead in most of the fighting, but this was not an effective military. Their resources, skills and leadership were inadequate. They lacked organization, training and most importantly, loyalty. Most of the soldiers were not trained professionals, but a part time militia of volunteers and conscripts. Their weapons were relatively crude and they were often not adequately clothed or fed. The Alliance was a fragmented array of factions from different regions and ethnic backgrounds. They had lost some of their key leaders, and were commanded by the tribal warlords of the old feudal Afghanistan. This was not a national military that had widespread support in its own homeland. It was a primitive militia that fought on horseback and pickup trucks. Fortunately, the Taliban were even less prepared and skilled for war, so they collapsed from the unrelenting pressure of the US air strikes.

The Afghan military (both sides) had no true allegiance. They traditionally tried to join the winning side, and often defected, just to survive the constant wars. Most Afghan Taliban soldiers were immediately released to return to their homes, still armed and radical. Taliban commanders bribed anti-Taliban Alliance officers to allow them to escape. Taliban "cabinet ministers" were released by the Afghans. Alliance forces allowed negotiations and surrenders with Taliban forces to go on for days, allowing leaders to escape. The Afghan culture of smugglers and warlords also provided easy escape alternatives for al Qaeda leaders. The network of fortified deep caves, some over 1000 feet deep, made al Qaeda core fighters and leadership difficult to find and attack. And they had many routes of escape. Thousands of Taliban and al Qaeda fighters escaped Afghanistan to Pakistan and Iran to fight another day. Afghan Alliance soldiers and commanders prayed for the safe passage and escape of Osama bin Laden, who was considered a Muslim hero in Afghanistan. When looking at the news reports of the anti-Taliban "victories", one had to ask: who is the enemy in this picture? After Taliban units surrendered to the Northern Alliance, it was declared "Yesterday my enemy—today my brother" as they were set free. The answer is *everyone* was America's enemy! The Afghan Taliban soldiers who were freed to return home established a resident terrorist, extremist population in the post war Afghan society.

America placed trust and dependence on its allies. But who were these allies really? The Afghans, whose warlords were more interested in their own power struggles after America set them free from the Taliban rule, who set up American forces to kill innocent civilians, who freed Taliban and al Qaeda fighters when they were captured, who assassinated leaders in the new Afghan government, *who are the Taliban*! Or the Pakistani's, who indoctrinated the Taliban in radical fundamentalist, militant Islam, supported them in their revolutionary takeover of Afghanistan, gave refuge and safe harbor to the Taliban and al Qaeda fighters and leaders who were driven from Afghanistan, and who kidnapped and murdered the Wall Street Journal Bureau Chief. These people were not part of the solution; they were part of the problem!

The US made a strategic decision in the war on terrorism to let the native armies fight the battles against terrorist organizations in their countries rather than using a massive attack by American forces. The American experience in Mogadishu had led them to try to avoid casualties in the future. This strategy was successful in the Gulf War and in Kosovo. But it could not be sustained in Afghanistan. At first, small units of Special Operations Forces were used to provide assistance and specific strikes with the support of air power and reconnaissance. There was limited use of US commando operations. Basically, the domestic forces did "the dirty work", but it turned out to be very inefficient, and often ineffective. American troops had to get involved in the ground war, even lead it, to hope to be successful. The Afghan militia was just not up to the task. And besides, this was really America's war! So, eventually, it required a major commitment of US forces to fight the war effectively; and the inevitable casualties followed. The dependency on Afghan forces to root out the Taliban and al Qaeda in the mountain regions of Tora Bora rather than US ground forces led to the failure to capture al Qaeda leadership and Osama bin Laden in particular. By the time the US and Allied forces took the lead in subsequent sweeps of the mountain regions, the enemy had escaped. America's "allies", Afghanistan and Pakistan, lost interest in chasing Taliban and al Qaeda. Afghanistan was trying to form a new government while coping with internal conflicts. Pakistan was preparing for war with India over Kashmir. So it diverted its armed forces and abandoned support of the US effort to hunt for Taliban and al Qaeda in the border region. America was left alone in a foreign and hostile land to continue its seemingly hopeless quest to track down the enemy.

## PERCEPTIONS

The massive US bombings and attacks with advanced weapons yielded mixed results at best. There were many questionable and missed targets in a land that was mostly made up of rocks, caves and ruble. Unfortunately, there is always some "collateral damage". Innocent civilians died and were injured because of mistakes and misguided bombings. And so did some allied soldiers. Arab groups and media generated anti-US propaganda. Civilian casualties in Afghanistan were the focus on news reports; not the fight against the Taliban or the search for al Qaeda. The US military operations were represented as a war against Islam, not the terrorists. In fact there was even a widespread rumor that the attacks of 911 were actually a Jewish conspiracy to turn the United States against the Arab world. And then there were the incidents when the US forces were given bad information about targets by local warlords. Instead of killing groups of al Qaeda soldiers, Afghan citizens died as victims of internal tribal politics. America was duped into slaughtering people it came to free. How do you think the locals felt when they saw US air attacks on a wedding party, a caravan of tribal leaders, a remote village, or a group of peasants? Hundreds were killed in these incidents and thousands of Afghan families claimed to have been innocent victims of American bombings. How do you think they felt about the US "liberation"? The bombing of Afghanistan by the United States eventually turned most, if not all, Afghans against America. Civilian casualties and extended military action in Afghanistan lost the support of Islamic Arab states as well as the Afghan people. Support for the USA in Europe gradually diminished as the bombing campaign dragged on. The decreasing moral support of military actions in Afghanistan was often heard in terms of "enough bombing—you are killing innocent people". And it certainly didn't help to hear the reports of atrocities committed by the Alliance troops, such as killing prisoners of war, Taliban sympathizers and collaborators. In most cases, these were actually old tribal enemies. There was also a growing resentment in Islamic countries and among Muslim minorities in other regions, including Europe, against the US treatment of the suspected al Qaeda terrorists who had been captured and detained in Guantanamo Bay. The hatred and militancy against the United States by the Muslim world, in general, became more pervasive and intense.

Even the attempted crackdown on organizations suspected of supporting the terrorists had an undesirable impact. By freezing the assets of hundreds of individuals and organizations, some innocent citizens and businesses in impoverished Arab countries were affected. As a result of mistaken links to al Qaeda, people and businesses lost access to their deposits and others lost jobs. This turned more Arabs against the United States.

The American military also had its shortcomings. There was a lack of coordination between the services, especially between the CIA and the military. There were also reports of micro-management and slow communications channels with the military headquarters back in the USA. Intelligence was inaccurate on locations of sites where the terrorists developed chemical and biological weapons. Past errors led American forces to believe they could not isolate targets accurately. The CIA had virtually no language and cultural skills to operate in Afghanistan. US agencies were totally dependent on local Afghans to provide intelligence support. Of course, the biggest disappointment was the failure to capture the leadership of the Taliban or al Qaeda. The American public began to lose its patience and, in some cases, its interest.

## HOPELESS NATION

The real problems emerged after the war. America fell into its traditional "trap" of peacekeeping and nation building; this time in Afghanistan. The US views of nation building solutions in Afghanistan were simplistic, even naïve. For a region made up of warring tribes that have not been at peace for 700 years, there is no simple solution. There certainly was no precedent for democracy in that region. Why should the US pay to rebuild a nation of people and culture that hate America? Afghanistan had no democratic heritage. It had a history of religious wars with monarchies and authoritarian rulers. It was a country of ethnic groups, tribes and clans. It had never been a "nation". After the war the feudal warlords returned to power and their fiefdoms in Afghanistan. And so did their record of corruption and tyrannical rule of the regions. There was a return of Taliban-era abuses of power and the population. Some of the warlords had military operations that were almost ten times the size of the International Security Force. There was even an organization of Islamic militants within Afghanistan that opposed a central government: the Hezb-i-Islami. How could anyone expect a new central government in Afghanistan to control its territories of fiefdoms and lawless regions?

The civilian situation in Afghanistan was essentially hopeless. There was no money or resources to build an infrastructure or to feed the indigent population. And they could not deal with the return of refugees who had fled to Pakistan, Iran, and other neighboring countries. There were more than five million of them; lost, no home, no refuge, and starving. They returned to poverty, devastation, and rekindled tribal wars. In addition, there were thousands of prisoners from the war. They could not continue to be held captive and fed, so most were freed. Afghanistan was an agricultural country. Most people had to live off of the land. After the war, the Afghan farmers resented the West, America and the UK in particular, for trying to force the destruction of opium crops. However, the opium merchants and the highest yield regions continued to operate. After all, the opium crop yielded ten times the payments the farmers received to destroy the crop. In the meantime, the warlords skimmed off portions of the opium and heroin that was captured. This was an impoverished and corrupt country before the war. How could Afghanistan be expected to cope with all of these new problems that just compounded their immense social and economical challenges?

The Northwest Frontier of Pakistan was also known as the "Tribal Zone" or "Lawless Region". It overlaps the Pakistan and Afghanistan border and was never controlled by a central government. It was a no man's land where "anything goes" and all authority is opposed. No outsiders were allowed into this region without specific permission, which usually came in the form of bribe money. This even applied to the Pakistani military. The area was controlled by tribal councils and leaders who reinforced a hatred for the West—Israel and the United States, in particular. This was a haven for Taliban, al Qaeda and their sympathizers. Terrorists and smugglers moved freely across the porous border. How do you tell the difference between a traditional Afghan or Pakistani tribal smuggler and a terrorist? They were all the same militant rebels. Weapons of mass destruction were available for sale, including biological materials from the former Soviet Union state of Ukraine. There were also Stinger missiles, the shoulder mounted anti-aircraft weapons that were supplied by the US CIA to the Afghan rebels to fight the Soviet Union in 1986. Hundreds of these were unaccounted for and were then trafficked by Afghan warlords to black markets and ultimately terrorist groups in Iran and Lebanon, as well as Afghanistan and the Pakistan arms market.

The return of the Warlords brought lawlessness and chaos, with continued instability aggravated by the presence of freed Taliban soldiers and commanders. The Warlords fought each other for power over regional fiefdoms and funded their campaigns through corruption, including currency manipulation. Traditional opposition groups, such as the Northern Tajiks and the Southern Pashtuns, tried to assume control of Afghanistan. Rival leaders were bombed and assassinated. Ethnic minorities were driven from their homes and villages. Northern tribes sought retribution from the former Taliban Pashtuns. Iran exerted influence and provided support in the northern and western regions where they shared a Shiite heritage. Extortion and robbery returned to the roads outside of the cities. Afghanistan was an armed camp with 10 million small arms in the hands of the population—or more than one gun for every adult male! This was a traditional source of pride in the region. The Pashtun creed was "a gun is the jewelry of a man"; and before the gun, there was the sword. The failure of the allied forces to disarm Afghanistan and later other radical Islamic states, proved to be a critical mistake.

The Alliance forces were never consolidated into a unified national military. Each of the warlords maintained their militia of thousands of troops. Guerrilla warfare broke out in the Southern region along the border with Pakistan, and in the mountain regions of the North and West. There was insurrection and internal power struggles with the new central government. Traditional rivalries between warlords and ethnic groups returned. The subsequent tribal wars led to more atrocities and violence against Afghan civilians, and a continuation of their long history of turmoil. After the defeat of the Taliban, Afghanistan returned to civil war, terrorism and the resurgence of Islamic militants, with renewed hatred of the United States. The Taliban and al Qaeda fighters regrouped as resistance fighters against the new Afghan regime and formed a coalition with renegade warlords to disrupt the new government. The International Security Force of fewer than 5000 was inadequate to keep the peace, control the warlords, and protect the country against the renegades and resistance. There was no chance for stability or central governance in Afghanistan. In addition to losing interest in pursuing escapees, there was a wide spread release of prisoners from the Afghan war due to inadequate resources to feed and keep them. And the traditional corruption even established a fee for release. For 1000 Pakistani rupees, or about US$16, Taliban and al Qaeda fighters were freed who still hated the USA, and were willing to continue to fight in the jihad. If the US had it to do over again, it would not let the local Alliance forces take the lead in both fighting and finding the Taliban and al Qaeda fighters. And it would not stay in Afghanistan to "stabilize the country" and get involved once again in "nation building".

## TERRORISM SURVIVES

The American leadership knew that Afghanistan was only the first step. Al Qaeda only used the Taliban for cover and protection. The air war and the defeats in Afghanistan, together with the international dragnet and arrests disrupted the Qaeda network, but only temporarily. They underestimated America's ability and resolve to retaliate, but it did not deter them from regrouping to try again. Al Qaeda developed a greater urgency and eventually became more aggressive. In time, they reconstituted the network. It became more organized and focused, with even better discipline and secretiveness. They moved their base of operations many times before, so they just dispersed to operate from other safe havens around the world to continue their "jihad" against America and the "west". They engaged terrorist networks in other regions. After the Afghan war, al Qaeda spread its terrorism to Pakistan and Tunisia where they targeted foreigners, including French and German citizens. Many of those that fought in Afghanistan were returning to their home bases and regrouping into the Qaeda cells. Many terrorists found support and refuge in Iran. Others had to travel farther. The Qaeda fleet of ships provided them with an ease of entry to many ports via containers, to smuggle weapons and even terrorists. Only a few percent of the containers were inspected even by US customs. But it was soon realized that "not all terrorism comes from al Qaeda". There were many other terrorist groups uncovered in countries such as Germany and England. They had loose ties and shared similar fanatical views. Some of them even received terrorist training in Afghanistan. America was not chasing a single enemy. Terrorism had many faces and forms throughout the world.

America learned the hard way that it can't introduce democracy into countries with a history of tribal warfare, such as Afghanistan, Somalia and Bosnia. There were also some countries that harbor terrorist organizations even though they condemn and crack down on terrorism. They didn't recognize territorial and political militant movements as terrorism; the Palestinian struggle with Israel in particular. The terrorists who escaped from Afghanistan and the global dragnet found new havens in uncontrolled states in Africa like the Congo, and in regions of the former Soviet Union, such as Chechnya in Russia, Abkhazia in Georgia, Nagorno-Karabakh in Azerbaijan and Transdneister in Moldova. And, of course, there was always refuge is the islands of Indonesia, among the largest Muslim population in the world. There were still too many places for the terrorist gangs to hide. The US placed hope in finding information about the escaped leaders, the secret cells and their future plans by interrogating the captives in Guantanamo as well as key individuals held elsewhere, like Abu Zubaydah. But they were trained to provide lies and misinformation, or they would just be uncooperative. This led to many false alarms and fruitless investigations. Poor communications between the US and European Intelligence also allowed some al Qaeda operatives and leaders in Europe to avoid capture. It was not going to be easy to prevent additional acts of terrorism.

Once the war in Afghanistan was "won", there was little interest by the "allies" to pursue "American objectives" any further, particularly to expand the war to other countries and targets, such as Iraq. The UN sanctions against terrorist states like Iraq had proven to be ineffective in stopping the flow of strategic and economic supplies. Without external scrutiny, Iraq was also able to build stockpiles of biological weapons including botulism and anthrax; by some estimates as much as 800 tons of deadly toxins. Iraq's resistance to international inspections, while lobbying to remove the sanctions just bought more time to rebuild its capabilities in weapons of mass destruction. The US would have to face this threat alone. Leaks to the media about the secret US plans to invade Iraq did not make it any easier.

While the turmoil evolved in Afghanistan, terrorist attacks and Israeli retribution continued in Palestine. The Palestinian leadership had no control over the militant organizations that seemed to have an unlimited supply of terrorists and suicide bombers. This terrorism persisted for more than 50 years and escalated even further. It didn't help that the current leaders of Palestine and Israel, Arafat and Sharon, had been personal enemies over that entire half century! New generations of Palestinians grew up to hate Israel and the United States. Arab states including Iran, Iraq and Syria provided arms and money to support the Palestinian terrorist organizations. The continued Palestinian terrorism undermined attempts at peaceful settlements between Israel and the Palestinian and Arab states. As a result, war broke out again in the

Middle East between Israel and the Palestinians together with their neighboring Arab allies. Now that the US was deeply involved in fighting terrorism around the globe as well as at home, what would it be willing to do in support of Israel? America had to make a choice. Diplomacy didn't work. The US had to consider getting involved in another war by fighting with Israel, providing military and intelligence support, or refusing to get involved. Could the US really abandon Israel after all these years? The Palestinian War could divert the attention, focus and resources of the US from its War on Terrorism.

On the domestic front, both the terrorist and criminal activity increased. US law enforcement refused to use gun purchases and background check records in the investigation of suspected terrorists in order to keep their commitment to the anti-gun control lobby. Obviously they were not yet serious about catching terrorists! The funding and coordination of security measures for state and local governments was just inadequate to get the job done. During this difficult time at home and abroad, the "Peace" movement emerged again. They just didn't get what was at risk. This was not Vietnam that was fighting someone else's questionable war in the name of democracy. This was an attack on America—and all it stood for! America found that altruism didn't work, not against uncompromising *evil*. Humanitarian aid, avoiding civilian casualties, tactical alliances, political compromises with the Middle East and Pakistan, and nation building just couldn't succeed. Terrorism needed to be fought aggressively and effectively on three fronts: Military—offensive and defensive; Political; and Cultural. It took the difficult lessons of the Early Years for America to decide to drastically change its approach.

# THE DEFENSE

America could no longer live with this Reign of Terror. The persistent attacks were devastating and left the country in shock. They threatened the economic stability of the nation as well as its lifestyle. But what was meant to break the spirit of the American pride and conviction, only served to strengthen the intensity of the resolve to defeat this nameless, godless enemy. A national priority was set to return "peace and security" at almost all costs. The President at the time said that "the most basic commitment of our government will be the security of our country". America focused on tightening security with all of its military, intelligence and law enforcement agencies.

## HOMELAND SECURITY

A National Homeland Security Agency was recommended in 1999, recognizing the risks America had already experienced from domestic terrorism. But it took the tragic events of 911 to bring the idea back to life. An Office of Homeland Security (OHS), and a Homeland Security Council was established to coordinate the security efforts and resources of all relevant federal agencies. However, it could not succeed in dealing with complex relationships of many diverse agencies, especially since it had no management or budget authority. Trying to coordinate the activities of many departments in a wide variety of government agencies was very frustrating. As the Administration became involved they realized that there was a lot of overlapping responsibilities, duplicate effort and poor communication. The early reorganizations and reforms in response to the revelations about intelligence failures were insufficient. There needed to be radical changes requiring a major reorganization and consolidation of the government bureaucracy. This made it necessary for the President to propose a cabinet level Department of Homeland Security that consolidated the resources of the Coast Guard, the Immigration and Naturalization Service (including the Border Patrol), the Customs Service, and the Secret Service. It was a good start, but it did not go far enough. It did not address all of critical roles and resources, took too long to implement, and just could not respond adequately to the Reign of Terror. Untangling the agency bureaucracies and congressional oversight committee structure proved to be a formidable task. Vested interests opposed proposals for dramatic changes and tried to undermine the Administration's efforts. An informal coalition of appointed officials, professional bureaucrats and congressional leaders fought against the changes until the President and the People had enough. The Reign of Terror proved that fragmented resources were not effective enough against this enemy. It was time put a real defense in place. The next step was to expand the scope of the Department of Homeland Security (DHS) to have domestic resources and power comparable to the Department of Defense. DHS would consolidate the key operational domestic security elements from all relevant agencies.

An early priority was, of course, the security of airports and commercial airlines. The government started by absorbing the 26,000 airport security guards to gain control of their operation. The Transportation Security Administration was formed to manage airport screening. However, it soon found that not only did this workforce and process need to be significantly improved, but also many other related operations needed to be integrated. It was going to require rigorous training, replacement and hiring as well as technology and procedural improvements to make airport security truly effective. The next step was to integrate all airline-related agencies; including the Federal Aviation Agency, the Air Marshals, and the Civil Air Patrol, together with airport security.

Border Security was another high priority. The number of daily border crossings into the USA was staggering; 1.3 million people, 340,000 vehicles, and 58,000 shipments. This was an immense security exposure. The responsibilities to manage the security of this process crossed a number of different federal agencies, each with its own priorities and interests. Initially there was substantial bureaucratic opposition to consolidation, but eventually they established a Border Security Agency within the DHS that contained the Border Patrol with its 10,000 agents, the Customs Service, the Immigration and Naturalization Service (INS), the Coast Guard, and part of the Agriculture Department that was responsible for quarantines.

The next step was law enforcement at the federal level. The Homeland Defense Agency was established to be a formidable defensive force comparable to the US military. The traditionalists in the Department of Defense proposed establishing a Northern Command, comparable to the other sectors that divided military responsibilities around the world. But the momentum for an autonomous and strong DHS was too great. Besides, the US military was prohibited from domestic law enforcement responsibilities or actions. So they built on the existing North American Aerospace Defense Command and combined the resources from the National Guard, the SWAT teams from the Bureau of Alcohol, Tobacco and Firearms, the US Federal Marshals, and the field operations of the Federal Bureau of Investigation. The National Guard alone was a force of 460,000 military personnel. However, the Guard was controlled by and responsible to the individual

States unless federalized. Up until then, the National Guard was only federalized by specific units for national emergencies. They would now form the core national resource for emergency response teams, civil defense support and anti-terrorism security duties. FBI agents would now focus on counter terrorism rather than Treasury Department related crime fighting, such as bank robberies and drug trafficking. That would be left to other federal agencies and state law enforcement authorities. Parts of the Army, Air Force, Coast Guard and National Guard were organized into a domestic anti-terrorist military command, called DAMCOM. It formed special teams to prevent and respond to each of the major types of terrorist threats—chemical, biological, radiation and, of course, bombing attacks.

It was also finally recognized that every branch of the government and, in fact, each of their major component parts, had its own security service. In addition to the well known and highly regarded Secret Service that protected the President of the United States, each cabinet level agency and Congress had their own version to assure the security of key government personnel and facilities. The Federal Security Service was established by consolidating these resources to improve the communication, coordination and overall level of effectiveness. A National Emergency Response Agency was formed by combining the Federal Emergency Management Agency (FEMA) with the Center for Disease Control and re-establishing the Civil Defense Corps. The fragmented domestic emergency staff functions from other departments were also consolidated into the new agency. One of its missions was to provide advanced training to emergency workers at the state and local level.

Finally, the US realized that it could no longer afford to have a fragmented intelligence community. There had been 13 autonomous government agencies involved in gathering intelligence on national security. The FBI, CIA, NSA and DOD each had operations responsible for monitoring foreign threats, but there was little communication and cooperation between them prior to 911. The National Intelligence Agency/NIA was formed to consolidate the resources and improve the effectiveness of one of the nation's most important defenses. In support of the NIA and the DHD in general, a new agency and federal mission was established to compile, control, manage and analyze vast amounts of data on individuals and organizations. The National Data Center was responsible for creating and maintaining a national ID system and central database for law enforcement agencies.

By reorganizing the federal agencies through consolidation and prioritization, the government was able to optimize its resources for more critical tasks. Homeland security was the national priority and it soon engaged a major portion of America's resources. The public realized that life was now all about survival, and they would have to invest heavily in protecting their freedom. Security, law enforcement and the military became careers of opportunity and growth in America. Government functions focused on Security and National Defense with the Executive Branch having operational responsibility, while the Congress played more of an oversight role. This was much like the relationship between a big business management team and their Board of Directors. Expanding and strengthening the powers of the Executive Branch and the President reversed the trend of increasing Congressional "assertiveness". This created some problems for the opposition party and the so-called liberal faction, but it was no true threat to the balance of power. The United States still had the most effective democracy in the world and now it would be more efficient.

## THE SECURITY CHALLENGE

The United States had extensive exposures to "foreigners" that put homeland security at risk. There were around *500 million legal* border crossings or entries into the USA each year. And there were *8 million illegal* aliens living in the country! Many were individuals who just stayed on after their visas expired. There were 300,000 violators of deportation orders and no one knew where they were! Among them were 6000 suspect Islamic men. The US was also a temporary home for hundreds of thousands of foreign students. America had the best schools in the world, which attracted students from many nations. These were "guests of the USA", not citizens. Over 500,000 student visas were issued every year with no control of when they leave or where they go, and no background checks conducted. Many of these students traveled frequently back and forth between the US and their homeland. Some were here on three month temporary visas for specialty training, including flight schools and war colleges. All they had to do was register for a course. The US even educated terrorists! It would not be easy to get the student visa program under control. The INS would need more agents to check for visa violations. There was resistance from the colleges that had become dependent on the revenue from foreign students. They were reluctant to risk the loss of such a lucrative market and reduce the use of their capacity. So in the balance of this security exposure was a "business consideration". It was time to get serious. The INS had to change its attitude that students pose no security risks. It began by developing a computer system to track foreign students in the USA. The "Student and Exchange Visitor Information System" (Sevis) would replace the ineffective INS paper process, but it was just a beginning of what would have to be done to eliminate this exposure.

This large exposure and lack of control was recognized too late to prevent 911. A number of hijackers were previously identified as suspected terrorists in the US and Europe. Despite some early leads that might have prevented the attacks, bureaucratic procedures and restrictions of law and rules hindered the authorities from following through on them. These were missed opportunities due to a lack of rigor in the system. It proved to be a tragic mistake. The INS even granted student visa status and eligibility to attend flight school in Florida to the two terrorist pilots of the airliners that crashed into the World Trade towers—six months after the attacks! The system was antiquated and the resources inadequate to do the job. Eventually, organization, procedures, rules and laws were all changed.

A major source of access to the US was through Canada. It had a liberal refugee policy and a relatively open border with the USA. There was also a rapid growth in Islamic centers in cities such as Montreal. Who knew how many terrorist cells were operating within a short driving distance to the North? Fortunately, the Millennium terrorist was caught at the border, but many others could have been crossing easily and routinely. The US had always been accessible by sea. Hundreds of foreign commercial ships entered US ports every day, collectively with thousands of crew members. Although the Coast Guard tried to screen all incoming ships after 911, it was not prepared to do the job effectively. It didn't have adequate resources to deal with the magnitude of the daily sea traffic. And it didn't have the equipment or training to inspect vessels for weapons of mass destruction. Although it tried to review crew lists, the Coast Guard did not have access to or communication with the databases of other agencies, such as the FBI, INS and Customs Service. And even these systems were antiquated with inefficient input and maintenance. The data was not accurate, complete, or up to date. So how were these agencies supposed to screen for terrorist suspects?

Social Security numbers had become a de facto standard for identity in the US. They were routinely used by government agencies and businesses to establish accounts and conduct transactions, but hundreds of thousands of Social Security numbers had been issued to non-citizens using fake documents. Many were used to obtain false IDs, which provided access to credit cards, bank accounts, and jobs—including known criminals and terrorists. The Social Security agency had not cross-checked new applications with INS records, and even when they started to, it was difficult to exchange useful data.

This required aggressive actions. First they had to break down the artificial barriers between government agencies and plug the "holes" in the system. In particular, they had to fix the weak enforcement in processes including drivers licenses, social security numbers, gun licenses, and cross checks with criminal and immigration records. Then they had to eliminate corruption and inefficiencies in the security agencies that had developed over many years and had been supported in part by the drug trade. Finally, they needed to develop new control systems to provide the ultimate remedy for the basic problems. The key to this was a new system for the "security of identity"; a comprehensive and fool proof positive ID for every one in America. It included photos, fingerprints, DNA, personal ID data and access to searchable national electronic files and databases. This computerized tracking and control process would not only assure a positive ID, but also track and control all entries and exits from the USA.

## SERIOUS DEFENSE

America decided that it had to be more committed to preventing terrorism than the terrorists were to create it. The US certainly had the advantage in terms of the resources and technology available. But it also realized that the terrorists had advantages as well, which collectively were even more formidable: unlimited targets; the surprise element; and the willingness to die while killing innocents. It was going to take some really serious defense to be effective against this kind of enemy.

After 911, travel security received a lot of focus and attention, but the initial actions were only the beginning of the significant changes that would be necessary to make public transportation secure. Airline security was, of course, a top priority and would never be the same. It had to be radically improved throughout the entire process. It started with ticketing. Airlines adopted a reservations only policy and had passenger lists pre-screened for known or suspected terrorists using FBI and INS files. This was especially important on flights from outside the USA. Airport security, of course, needed a lot of work to improve the screening of passengers and cargo. This included the inspection of all personal baggage, both carry-on and checked, requiring more security personnel as well as technology. Bags were matched with all legs of a trip. But the US did not have a process to prevent bombs from checked baggage. Dogs were used to check luggage and aircraft for explosives until new technology was deployed to more effectively screen baggage for explosives. It would require thousands of machines to screen the baggage at all the US airports for explosives. Only a few hundred were ordered and installed at the major airports until a more advanced technology was developed that provided higher throughput and greater accuracy. Metal detectors were not foolproof for screening individuals and their personal carryon luggage. They couldn't detect plastics such as explosives or even plastic weapons. It was still possible for someone to have a functional knife made of plastic that could also get through X-ray machines, especially if it was fashioned to look like, or be embedded in ordinary personal items—like a comb. This made the personal screening process critical. Every passenger had to have a positive ID. And the screening process had to be "intelligent", not frivolous or just for show. A profiling system was developed to focus on more rigorous screening of specific passengers who might pose some risk. This required skilled interrogation and a new level of security personnel that had previously been developed as an effective methodology by Israel's El Al airline. Then came the on board security. Cockpits were secured and armed. This required a retrofit of all the cockpit doors and training of the cockpit personnel. Surveillance cameras provided a continuous view of the cabin from the cockpit. Air Marshals were assigned to travel on every major flight. Since it was not possible to cover all of the tens of thousands of daily commercial flights, it was decided to staff all flights by full size jet aircraft from major airports. In addition, there was also random coverage of other flights from other airports. Terrorists then knew that there would always be a possibility of an armed professional Air Marshall on any commercial flight. Eventually advanced ticketing and registered travel documents were required for all major types of public transportation; airlines, railroads and ships. Frequent travelers were able to obtain travel "permits" or clearances to ease their screening process, but the Registered Passenger Program required rigorous background checking and approvals. Travel became a privilege, not a freedom. The rigors of security eliminated any sense of luxury or enjoyment from public transportation. This was a price that had to be paid.

It soon became clear that tighter security controls on the public transportation carriers and passengers was not enough. There were also thousands of service workers with easy access to areas that posed a security risk. This was particularly true for maintenance and catering personnel. A patient terrorist would not find it difficult to obtain a job for one of these services that in many cases do not require special skills or experience. A service worker could easily plant a bomb on an airplane, train, bus or ship. There were also enough examples to prove how easy it would be to impersonate one of these service workers. Something had to be done to plug this hole. The Department of Transportation started by cracking down on illegal aliens working at airports after 911. Eventually, all public transportation organizations were required to screen existing and prospective employees and contractors with rigorous background checks and positive IDs. This also rooted out many illegal aliens and undocumented workers.

One of the top priorities was to establish a comprehensive positive identification system that would protect lawful American citizens and aid law enforcement authorities in locating criminals and terrorists. There was much interest in a "national ID", but the early efforts to develop a uniform driver's license proved to be inadequate although it was a start. It was finally decided that the National ID should be the primary identification for all US citizens and visitors. Driver's licenses, passports and private security badges could then be based on it. A "Smart Card" technology was developed using multiple electronic identification methods tied to a central national database. The photograph was also captured as an electronic file of the image and had to be updated every five years. The embedded chip also included biometric data; fingerprints, an Iris image, a facial scan and DNA code. It also held other key personal identification data including social security number, birth date and place, citizenship and blood type. Developing the technology for this smart ID card was the easy part. Compiling correct verifiable data on all Americans was a huge challenge. Individuals had many identifications, and sometimes multiple ones. For most people, there were at least driver's licenses, credit cards, and social security numbers. It took years full of obstacles and significant costs, but it got done. The National ID became the primary control of American citizenship.

The establishment of national databases to support the National ID system was a massive project that involved many government agencies at the federal and state levels. There was already a lot of data available on everyone in the USA, but it was not accessible or integrated for the authorities to use. Of course, this was not just a technical or resource issue. It was also a very sensitive and controversial privacy issue. But national security prevailed and the project was supported. The first

priority was to focus on criminals as well as known and suspected terrorists. This, of course, would include the FBI's "most wanted" list and
extensive federal criminal database. That was followed by data on all
citizens, residents and visitors through the new National ID system,
together with web based links to international databases. The National
Database was eventually linked by a broadband wireless network providing efficient, real time access by law enforcement authorities across
the country. In addition to the new central database of individuals,
access was developed to all the major databases and records systems at
the federal, state and local levels, including key business systems, credit
and bank records in particular. This was a massive amount of data.
Many databases already existed, they just needed software, data communications, and storage systems to link, integrate and search them.
The key to making it useful was data mining tools to search and com-
pare inter-agency files and multiple databases. There were records on
most individuals from many sources, such as credit, police, prison, FBI,
INS, medical, military, and taxes at the federal, state and local levels.
And there were also the vast numbers of transactions of individuals,
including banking, travel, purchases and tax payments.

The Terrorist Profiling System was built on existing relational database and data mining technologies similar to those that were already
used for tracking credit card fraud. Existing federal agency databases
were integrated, and privacy laws were relaxed to give government
access to commercially available personnel data, such as credit cards,
phones, bank transactions, and travel. This system gave the authorities
extensive capabilities to detect and track potential terrorists, and it also
helped find all types of criminals. Automated systems were used to
replace and supplement human monitors, including suspicious movements. Searches could be made routinely for links to the activities and
locations of individuals under suspicion. It could be used for background checks for business and government employment. Eventually,

*everyone* was screened and tracked. The National Database project was both a challenge and a boom to the Information Technology industry. Concerns were raised about privacy and civil liberties, however, the privacy of Americans had already been compromised by increasingly intrusive government and business practices for years. And who was really concerned about protecting criminal behavior?

Advanced security technology was the key to providing effective tools for protecting America at all levels. The government engaged the high tech industry to apply and invent advanced technologies to prevent terrorism, just as it had in the past to support the development of military weapons. Federal spending in this area would grow beyond the initial $60 billion allocated. Some agencies became a source of venture capital to stimulate the high tech sector. The CIA started by establishing a firm called "In-Q-Tel" that began investing more than $30 million a year in internet start-ups. This was just a beginning as the government's security agencies became more aggressive in pursuing technology solutions.

Since finding terrorists presented a challenge that was similar to looking for a needle in a haystack, the traditional labor intensive approaches were just not adequate. America decided that it needed high tech assurance of its security, even if it had to sacrifice some of its freedoms. The new field of biometric sensors presented a variety of sophisticated tools for the law enforcement community. Fingerprints could be stored and read electronically. Retina imaging made positive identification possible with eye scans, and facial scans could be more effective than mug shots and lineups. Surveillance security was revolutionized. Facial recognition systems were tied to databases of criminals and suspects to monitor public places. Camera surveillance systems were installed at airports, stadiums, monuments and transportation centers. They became a routine practice at major events such as the Olympics. This, of course, raised the specter of "Big Brother" for some, but it was not without precedent. A closed circuit TV surveillance system was used in London in response to IRA bombings in 1993 and 1994. It was so effective in deterring terrorists as well as providing the added benefit of crime prevention, that it spread throughout the UK in all major metro areas. Advances in the development of biometric recognition technology, particularly with respect to speed and accuracy, made high tech surveillance practical on a large scale. And the positive identification capabilities of electronic fingerprints and retinal scans provided efficient tools for controlled access to secure facilities in both the public and private sector. No one could travel or operate in the business world and be anonymous. That was not a big price for law biding citizens to pay for security.

Surveillance capability was literally elevated to new levels by advanced satellite imaging and navigational technologies. Using ultra-sensitive, high resolution satellite surveillance photography together with Global Positioning Systems made it possible to locate the origins of cell phone calls and search for terrorist locations. Multi-spectral imaging technologies were employed, including X-ray, infra red, and ultra violet, in addition to optical photography. Top secret US government systems were capable of detecting objects from space that were less than five inches in diameter. They could look at anyone and anything, anywhere.

New technology was also applied to another area of conventional surveillance—communications. Monitoring phone calls and email from and to potentially risky sources became a key part of national security. All types of communication were involved; email, telephone via land lines, cell phone and Internet surfing. The detection and eavesdropping of suspects became an automated electronic process using advanced surveillance technologies. The "CARNIVORE" system could scan and read emails. "ECHELON" was a powerful wiretapping device to monitor cell phones, faxes and email. There was even a technology to search for hidden patterns inserted in picture or music files on the Internet used by terrorists to communicate secret messages. This was called "Steganography analysis" from the Greek for hidden writing. People soon realized that someone was always listening.

Of course, a top priority for the security strategy was to prevent bio terrorism. It took years to get to a state of adequate readiness. There were exposures everywhere; mail, water supplies, high density population centers, public transportation and major events. Hazardous materials could be hauled by trucks or sprayed from crop dusting airplanes. The early incidents focused attention on mail security. Personnel protection actions included decontamination and sterilization to kill "germs" with electron beams, cobalt source radiation and X-rays. New stringent mail handling controls were imposed. Return addresses were required on all mail. Mail and packages dropped off at Post Offices required signatures with positive ID. However, the greatest improvement in mail safety was from the alternatives. Electronic communications became the primary mode for private and commercial mail. "Junk mail" was eliminated. Businesses and individuals did their transactions online using eCommerce tools. Physical mail was restricted. What was left was suspect and inspected. Post cards, open mail and clear envelopes replaced most traditional envelopes. Overseas mail was impounded, tested and inspected. Security measures changed the economics and modes of communication. The mission and technology of the US Postal Service was revolutionized. The new US Communication Service provided more efficient and secure solutions for the needs of both the public and private sector.

To be prepared for biological attacks, national stockpiles were established for antibiotics and vaccines. Emergency distribution and delivery systems were developed to assure rapid access to these stockpiles whenever and wherever they were needed. When the threats increased and the attacks continued, it was decided to implement a national program of mass vaccinations for anthrax and smallpox. The costs and risks were not considered too great to seek universal protection. Smallpox vaccinations came with risks of injury and even death; as many as a few hundred for every million people exposed. America had accepted these odds in the past and was willing to again. At the same time, new technologies were deployed to screen for explosives and bio/chemical sources. Genetic coding of biohazards provided a tool for detecting biological and chemical contaminants, such as anthrax, with air monitoring devices. Hazardous material emergency response groups, called "Hama Teams", were trained and equipped to react quickly with the latest technologies for detection, analysis, treatment and cleanup. This was a new area of defense, perhaps even more important than conventional weapons.

Some of the most dangerous sources of hazardous materials were already under the control of federal agencies, but the security was inadequate to prevent terrorists from gaining access to them. There was more than 50,000 tons of radioactive waste from nuclear power plants that needed to be disposed of and buried. This source of potentially lethal material was distributed between more than 100 power plant facilities in the USA, with varying levels of security control. The threat of terrorism finally convinced the government to act on this problem that had been building for decades. Heightened concerns for nuclear security eventually justified an investment of more than $40 billion for the consolidation and disposal of these nuclear wastes in a facility in Yucca Mountain, Nevada. Local concerns about having such a facility in their "backyard" had to take a back seat to national security. It was also realized that the extensive network of government supported laboratories was a significant source of potentially dangerous biological and radioactive materials. The security controls at these federal, university and private labs had to be substantially improved. Hazardous materials became a priority of national security; not just an environmental and economical problem.

The line between national and private security disappeared. Significant investments were required by law enforcement, security and military services for detection and protection equipment, and personnel training. The routine practices of security for office buildings changed dramatically. This affected not just the procedural and operational aspects, but also the physical and technical aspects of the facilities. Street barriers, bullet and bomb proof partitions, sophisticated monitoring systems and emergency response resources became an integral part of all major buildings. Advanced screening and surveillance technologies were used everywhere. New and remodeled buildings even made architectural changes to improve security. The business world had to become fortified.

The borders of the USA and, in fact, the Americas in general, were notoriously porous. Significant investments had to be made to secure them. To be effective, it would take more than an increase in resources. The application of advanced technologies would also provide solutions here. Night vision goggles and long range scanning were supplemented with motion sensors and infra-red barrier alarms. Unmanned, robotic patrol vehicles and surveillance aircraft proved to be much more practical than just adding more border guards. For critical areas that were also difficult to patrol, a new high tech invisible fence was deployed that included a non-lethal microwave weapon, and of course, the positive ID system and integrated national database would finally make screening efficient.

The government also decided to restrict public access to scientific documents that may be of use to terrorists. A wide variety of technical information had been readily available on the design and production of biological, chemical and nuclear weapons. Ironically, the US government was helping to educate potential terrorists on how to prepare weapons of mass destruction! This door was finally closed, but not without some controversy. It was a trade off for security. Restricting the traditional open information exchange among the scientific community would hinder advances in research and discovery. A slower pace of innovation would not be a great sacrifice.

New security controls were developed for the nation's leaders, with particular focus on the line of succession to the Presidency and the Cabinet. Secure locations and alternate offices were established for all key personnel. There were restrictions on who could travel and meet together. Their movements were under constant surveillance and control. There were no longer advanced announcements on their travel and formal engagements. Tele- and video conference meetings were routine. Electronics became the preferred mode for communications, especially television and the Internet. Top secret plans were developed to respond to "doomsday scenarios", including maintaining a "shadow government" operating in secure underground facilities to take control if and when they are needed.

The approach to national security took on a new level of intensity. It was no longer "business as usual". The major holes in the system had to be plugged, and it took some tough actions to get the job done. The US government finally had to get serious! There was no place anymore for the "bleeding heart liberals" or featherbedding bureaucrats that traditionally stood in the way of tough law enforcement. The crackdown was based on common sense. Security came first. The Foreign Student Visa Program, which had virtually no controls, was shut down. Restrictions and inspections were imposed on all foreign aircraft and ships. All charities and organizations operating in the USA that supported, even

potentially, terrorist (or even any) foreign state were shut down—
including support for Israel! Law enforcement teams at the federal, state
and local levels worked together to shut down and clean-out the com-
pounds and mosques of radical fundamentalist groups. This was
applied to all anti-American and paramilitary groups, not just Muslim.
Eventually all anti-American militants were arrested and offered three
alternatives: jail, restricted parole, or deportation.

The law enforcement community had to make changes in the skills
and tools required to do the job. There was an increased focus on
"Human Intelligence" at the international, national and local levels. The
intelligence agencies recognized that they needed to use "bad guys" to
catch bad guys. The "covert" activities of the CIA were increased and
expanded including the infiltration and interrogation of terrorist
groups. The "spy" activities and support services of the CIA and FBI
were coordinated to focus on terrorist organizations "of global reach".
Terrorist leaders were targeted and hunted down. Some were captured
with the help of local authorities, both within and outside the USA.
Others were set up for attacks and even assassination. It was not unlike
the secret tactics during the years of the "cold war" against communism.
This was a new and continuing phase of the war on terrorism.

# UNIFICATION

The surge in patriotism that followed 911 evolved into something greater that eventually reshaped the nation and its politics. This new feeling of nationalism started by institutionalizing flags and anthems at all events and all public facilities. "God Bless America" was the pervasive expression of patriotism. There were soon growing movements that rallied around calls for "America First" and "America for American Independence". The priority role for federal government became a focus on self protection and survival. American politicians finally decided to stop wasting time and money fighting among themselves. Americans wanted to "get rid of all the crazies". Most, and probably almost all, Americans were basically good, hard working people. But there was an element of criminals, crazies, and basically bad people that the "good Americans" decided they would no longer tolerate. The conventional politics of America developed into a kind of zero tolerance conservatism.

## THE PURGE

America decided that it could not control its security unless it significantly increased its control of the population. It could not continue to be an open society. A process of purging began. The initial slowdown on visa applications by Arabs was not enough to stop the flow of potential terrorists. There needed to be strictly enforced exclusions. It started with new rules for travel and immigration. America began to isolate itself. American citizens who continued to travel outside the USA were restricted to controlled territories and, even then, considered at high risk. Security alliances were established with other key, closely related countries who were trying to become more secure states. Businesses now had to rely on foreign nationals to staff and run their operations outside the USA, and only in those acceptable controlled territories and states. Americans were no longer the "world tourist class". Foreign tourism in the USA was severely restricted, as was immigration. America no longer provided asylum or political refuge; even to "the tired and the poor". Foreign Students were at first restricted and then eliminated. Immigration was only permitted from "approved" countries and individuals were required to have relatives, references and financial support before being considered as acceptable candidates to enter the country. America eventually closed its borders. Only citizens of the "Americas" were allowed to stay. Illegal aliens were tracked down and deported. Resident aliens and workers were given the option to apply for citizenship—or leave.

Law enforcement was, of course, critical to the success of the nation's security strategy. There was a need to make radical legal changes to support the objectives of preventing terrorism and serious crime. Surveillance was pervasive. Eavesdropping became acceptable and commonplace. Even lawyer-client phone calls and prison conversations were fair game. Positive IDs and permits were required for public transportation. The allowable detention period for non-citizens was extended from 24 hours to five days. Banking restrictions on access to and freezing of accounts were eased. The laws had been more restrictive on protecting the rights of terrorists than on drug traffickers. It was time to put things in the proper perspective when it came to public security.

Laws dealing with search and interrogation also had to be addressed. Law enforcement authorities needed more flexibility when investigating suspected or potential terrorists. Search, seizure and interrogation became commonplace. Strip searches were conducted without challenge by the courts, and it took some court reversals on civil liberties for security considerations to prevail when it came to profiling. Specific IDs and profile characteristics were developed for all suspects and wanted persons in the National Database. Profiling was no longer a bad word. It was a practical tool to identify dangerous suspects. After all, what is wrong with objectively describing the known characteristics of the criminals you are trying to find? Extreme pressure was exerted on suspected terrorists, especially leaders of cells and known terrorist organizations. Interrogations were supplemented by forced lie detection techniques, including the use of chemicals and truth serum. Many advocated using torture, and some of the most serious cases in the hands of federal authorities resorted to it. They were dealing with fanatical killers, not rational, innocent citizens. A lot was learned from the experience with al Qaeda captives held at the Guantanamo Bay military base in Cuba. These were not the typical military prisoners of war. They had no national allegiance or code of conduct. New rules were required for this new breed of criminal.

Military tribunals and inquisitions replaced the criminal court system when it came to terrorism. Individuals captured in the US as suspects for domestic terrorism were treated as "enemy combatants" with restricted legal rights. New stricter and stronger guidelines were developed on sentences for terrorists, including the death penalty. Executions were routinely used for convicted Taliban and al Qaeda leaders. This new "get tough" approach was eventually also applied to violent crime convictions. There were new limitations on appeals and the time that convicts could spend on death row. The time when convicted murderers could stay in prison for decades was over. And no leniency was given for extremist, anti-American groups in the United States. Treason returned as a legal "ethic". There were new laws and penalties applied to cases involving traitors. American law even adopted a "zero tolerance" policy for crimes that take advantage of terrorist situations. This was a time for "no-nonsense justice". No more of being "not guilty" of capital crimes when proven guilty by the facts. Insanity or stress was not an excuse for murder. Rights violations or technicalities were not opportunities to free guilty criminals. Military justice made a lot of sense.

Of course there was a lot of opposition from civil liberties groups about the "constitutional rights" of all suspects and convicts. Law enforcement pushed the limits of the Constitution as well as established federal laws in its pursuit of counter terrorism measures. The detention of suspects was often extended and secret. Names of detainees were withheld for security reasons. Domestic spying of suspect individuals and organizations used all of the weapons in the intelligence arsenal: eavesdropping, wiretapping, investigation, interrogation, search and seizure. America decided to sacrifice some of its privacy and civil liberties for security. Many of the basic rights, which perhaps had been somewhat extreme in detail, but still uniquely American, were compromised. There was no doubt that traditional freedoms were being reduced and restricted, but restrictions of civil liberties in wartime had many precedents. What are the fundamental rights of a free people? Historically, some rights varied with time and experience. Laws were often changed by events and new realities. There needed to be a balance between civil liberty rights and security. And besides, who says the US Constitution was designed to protect the rights of foreign terrorists who commit war crimes against America? In wartime, military law often took precedence over civil justice. However, some questioned when does the "war" end? America had no more patience for "bleeding hearts". So-called human rights organizations claimed inhumane treatment of US prisoners from the Afghan war who were held in Guantanamo. In fact, they were "illegal combatants"; foreigners fighting in another nation's war, not controlled by a legitimate national government, and not applicable to the Geneva Convention or the US Constitution. And they were suicidal terrorists, not soldiers. However, they were still treated humanely in high security military prison conditions, and it was much better treatment than they deserved or that the Taliban afforded to Afghans. Like, for example, when they summarily executed men and women in public stadiums for minor offenses. The debate about the status of US captured Taliban and al Qaeda prisoners in terms of their legal rights and humane treatment relative to the Geneva Convention was mostly an issue in other countries not directly affected by 911. America had to have its own justice.

The US Intelligence community had been severely criticized for not detecting the operations of the terrorist network prior to the 911 attacks. And they did not have the language and cultural skills to infiltrate and interrogate al Qaeda or the Taliban. These agencies had also been constrained from covert operations, so the leadership of known terrorist organizations and the states that supported global terrorism were never hunted. That all changed when the American Intelligence agencies were consolidated. It took years to recruit and develop the necessary skills, but covert operations against terrorist groups became a high priority—including assassinations.

Perhaps the biggest legal challenge came with gun control in America. After 911, there was a significant increase in gun purchases and first time ownership. This became a major problem for law enforcement agencies. America had always been known for its relative ease of access to guns by the public, but it eventually seemed like "everyone was armed". As a natural extension of the security program, America finally decided it needed to do something serious about guns. Any restrictions on gun ownership had been strongly opposed for many years by the powerful gun lobby. But people finally realized that this large inventory of guns threatened the peace, safety and security of the nation. It started with tough new federal laws on the possession and use of weapons by criminals. Mandatory sentences were imposed, including death for murderers using guns as weapons. The federal law and program on gun control was expanded to require licenses and registration for all hunting weapons and individuals. "Authorized" hunters were screened, trained, tested, registered and tracked. Eventually, all handguns and non-hunting weapons were confiscated and outlawed. When the Federation was formed, these laws were introduced to all American countries. This was seen by some to be a violation of constitutional rights, but by most people as the final demise of the "wild west" image of America. After all, the new restrictions were really not much more severe than had already existed in a number of other developed western countries. It took years to fully implement the program, but America finally "disarmed" its citizens.

## THE ECONOMY

A severe recession evolved out of the economic slowdown America had been experiencing when it was further impacted by 911 and its aftermath. It was estimated that the direct economic impact of 911 exceeded $150 billion. The Reign of Terror caused even more economic disruption and havoc to many sectors. Costs increased for transportation, security, insurance, and information technology. Millions of jobs and billions in revenue were lost in key industries, such as airlines and aircraft, automotive, travel and services, entertainment and restaurants, and the meetings, events and conventions industry. Cut backs in capital investment delayed a recovery of the economy. The federal government was forced to bail out and control some of the most seriously impacted industries, including airlines, insurance and the Postal Service. The federal economic stimulus, together with the cost of the war and recovery, drove the country back into deficit spending and increased the national debt. Most government budgets at federal, state and local levels went rapidly from surplus to deficits after 911. The scandals and bankruptcies of big business caused a panic in the stock market and people lost their investments. America faced a challenge of how to stimulate an economy that was already stagnating, then severely impacted, while waging a war of undetermined size and scope.

The country needed to focus on security, safety, stability and control. To do that, government spending at the federal and state levels had to be re-prioritized as well as increased. It was not that there wasn't enough money available. The total net cost of the US federal government at the time was approximately $2.5 trillion! But most of it was committed to established and legislated programs. It would be very difficult to make radical changes to the budget. The federal bureaucracy and congressional politics were very protective of their territories and "entitlements". But something had to be done to finance the war on terrorism while re-building a stable and secure nation. The necessary increases in spending could not all come from new tax revenue. Significant tax increases would only drive the economy into a deeper depression.

The national defense comprised almost 20% of the budget, at around $400 billion. However, it needed to be significantly increased to improve military readiness, for rapid and emergency response. The first area to get scrutiny was the largest; human resources. That was more than 50% of the budget, or about $1.3 trillion. There had to be some opportunities to decrease spending. The targets included "income security", education and training. Physical resources were around 6% of the budget, or $200 billion. Opportunities were found to decrease spending on natural resources, the environment, commerce and transportation. And there was another $200 billion being spent on "Other Functions" where decreases were made in agriculture, international affairs and aid.

But there also needed to be increases for the "administration of justice", science and technology and space. Federal spending on Research and Development was well over $100 billion per year, so there was a capability for significant investments in technology, but the R&D budgets would have to be reprioritized and the waste reduced to a minimum. This was not an easy puzzle to solve. It took a new resolve by politicians recognizing the true interest of the public in protecting America. There was no longer room for "sacred cows" or unnecessary "pork barrel" projects. A lot of tough decisions were eventually made to finance the "Fortress". There were drastic reductions in "non-strategic" programs, such as foreign aid and domestic social and economic programs. America cut off all financial and military aid; especially the "offsets" that had been used to support local foreign economic development interests. They also stopped the bailouts and loan forgiveness as well as the support of the IMF, the UN and NATO. America basically cut off the money and weapons it had been supplying to the Rest Of the World— what it had been putting into the hands of friends as well as enemies; peacekeepers and terrorists. The United States had been feeding war and terrorism, and it had to stop.

These actions freed up a lot of money to redirect for internal priorities. There was also a major commitment to stop waste by reducing the unnecessary and inefficient bureaucratic overhead of government. The targets were the notoriously slow processes, political perks, redundancies, and uncontrolled waste and abuse in general. No one really knew how much waste there was in government spending, but most believed it was a lot; maybe 25% or possibly even as much as 50%. The President set an "efficiency challenge" of 10%, which would save $250 billion a year if achieved. When the government tried to operate more like a responsible business there was a lot more money made available to invest in building the Fortress.

It was also time to face some tough decisions on taxes. There was finally a crackdown on tax avoiders; individuals and corporations. Why should the honest, middle class workers and good corporate citizens carry the burden for those who found ways around the system? The individuals and companies that had moved their assets and legal entities off shore to reduce their tax obligations would have to decide whether they wanted to be part of America or not. You would no longer be able to have it both ways. If you wanted to have the privileges and protection of being an American citizen or company, you would have to share the tax burden. That doesn't really sound so radical does it? And there would be more equitable tax rates. Everyone and every organization would have to pay something. If you are going to benefit from membership in the "club", then you should pay the dues. Even "not-for-profit" organizations, that in many cases make more money than conventional medium size businesses, would have to pay their fair share of taxes. This also meant including Native American (Indian) businesses, such as casinos and oil wells.

The dramatic increase in spending on defense and security created a new "military-industrial complex" driven by homeland security and anti-terrorism technologies. This eventually proved to be a stimulus to the economy as well as technology development, just as it had during the years of prior major wars, but it came at a price. Social programs became a secondary priority at the federal level. The overall cost of government increased, and so did the tax burden to support it. It was expensive to create a secure state.

## THE SHIELD

Once America decided to aggressively strike out against its enemies while bolstering its domestic security, it needed to assure adequate protection of the country. You cannot have an effective "Fortress" without building an impenetrable "Shield". Although the USA was the last true "superpower", its defense systems were aging. To deal with the potential threats of modern warfare as well as global terrorism, it was necessary to invest heavily to upgrade and expand all aspects of its defense.

The United States was always considered to be at the leading edge of technology, but to assure its security, it adopted a national strategy of domination and exploitation of technology. It started by using existing advanced technologies for innovative approaches to counterterrorism. There was a major focus on countermeasures against weapons of mass destruction and disruption such as chemical, biological, radiation, nuclear, and information technology, or cyber terrorism. A project was organized to develop new applications and tools. They recruited key skills and resources from industry, government laboratories, research institutes, and universities. The National Counterterrorism Technology Center was established to coordinate and organize this effort across many agencies. The project included research and development as well as application. Technology partnerships were established with other countries and major companies. It was a long term project to address the continued development of new and more advanced terrorist threats, weapons and sources. This was not just a quick fix for a current problem.

America took advantage of its strength and resolve to obtain the resources and skills it needed to get the job done. It pursued other nations, such as Russia and England that had advanced technology capabilities, but could not afford to invest further in them. Technologies were obtained through licenses, product acquisitions, and development contracts. Key people in science, technology and intelligence were recruited worldwide to work in America. There were major purchases and development contracts for unique weapons and defense systems. And long term contracts for strategic resources; oil, gas, and precious metals in particular.

America acted to make sure that it continued to dominate the air, the oceans, and outer space. The US had, for years, advocated the development of an advanced missile defense system. This "Star Wars" scenario was opposed by many for both its cost and its threat of escalating a world arms race. 911 changed the domestic attitude. It started with the US withdrawal from the Anti-Ballistic Missile Treaty. This led the way for the development of a new generation of offensive and defensive missile systems and aircraft. Advanced high speed ground based missiles could intercept short range missiles fired by renegade states. A new fleet of advanced unmanned aircraft equipped with weapons was deployed for surveillance missions. Outer space became the sole domain of America. It developed a state-of-the-art satellite system for the surveillance of all forms of communications as well as very high resolution photography and radar imaging. A network of "Killer Satellites" with high power laser weapons provided a space-based defense against enemy missiles. There was also a major build-up in new nuclear weapons. To support the program, the United States invested in the recycling and reprocessing of spent nuclear fuel as a source of critical Plutonium.

To complete the Shield, America built a "high tech" military around precision weapons, unpiloted aircraft, and high tech battlefield communications using advanced wireless technologies. The innovation that had been focused for decades on the commercial and consumer sector was redirected to national security. A new generation of defense equipment and systems emerged. There was no country operating in the same century of warfare technology as the United States.

## INDEPENDENCE

For America to build the Fortress, it had to eliminate its dependencies on other countries. Although Americans always liked to think that they were unique in the world and had everything, over the years American growth and development actually fostered a global dependency on some basic resources. Since America could no longer depend on long term trade and economic relationships in a world of unrest, America decided to invest in its independence.

The greatest dependency and, as a result, the most critical resource at risk, was energy. The American economy and way of life grew to depend on a continuously growing demand for energy that could always be satisfied at reasonable costs. The country learned the hard way several times that energy supplies were not always dependable. The historical dependence of the industrialized countries on the Middle East for a large portion of their oil supply had caused problems in the past and became an unacceptable, even implausible situation in the new world environment. It was time for the US to stop being held hostage to Arab oil. Even though Europe and Japan had a greater dependence on oil from the Middle East, America's ties to the global economy had allowed it to be manipulated by the OPEC cartel.

Fortunately, at the time, the US Administration could draw upon extensive experience in the energy industry to formulate and execute an aggressive strategy. Project "Energy Independence" was multi-faceted and comprehensive. It addressed all the key aspects of the challenge. The short term solution to eliminating the dependency on Middle East oil was to establish strategic contracts with alternate sources such as Mexico, Canada, South America/Venezula, Russia, and Norway. Collectively, these countries actually had a larger production capability than the Middle East and, of course, were generally more politically aligned with the USA. The strategic alliance with Russia was particularly important and unique. Russia was one of the largest producers of oil in the world, comparable to Saudi Arabia, and led the world in gas reserves. It desperately needed cash to redevelop its struggling economy. The new oil supply treaty with Russia not only guaranteed a significant long term supply for America, but it led to the development of a pipeline between Siberia and Alaska, creating the world's largest network of oil and gas delivery systems. In conjunction with these new and expanded sources of supply, the United States filled and expanded its strategic reserves to provide improved protection from short term disruptions.

The major thrust of the long-term solutions was an aggressive invest-ment in oil and gas exploration to exploit the untapped resources of North and South America. Since about two-thirds of the oil consumed by the US at the time actually came from the "Americas" (US, Canada, Venezuela and Mexico), it was not an unrealistic goal. The plan included the development of Arctic resources in the USA and Canada together with new pipelines. The Congress gave up its opposition to oil and gas exploration in the Arctic National Wildlife Refuge when it finally realized that energy independence must take precedence over questionable environmental concerns. And the coastal states relaxed their restrictions on off-shore drilling. There was also the development and expansion of oil and gas supplies from Latin America, which pro-vided much needed capital for those struggling economies. Since the USA was already considered the "Saudi Arabia of Coal", it was able to expand its production with relative ease using a balance of technology and regulatory relief. Along with the exploitation of traditional resources, alternate fuels and energy sources now became much more attractive and economically feasible. For example, coal bed methane was a significant source of natural gas from deep deposits of coal in the western United States and Canada. Ethanol produced from surplus corn crops became an economical gasoline supplement. Fuel cells began to find wide spread practical applications, and windmill farms were developed in the arctic, coastal waters, and the Great Plains.

Of course, the energy strategy would not be complete without an investment in conservation. This actually proved to be the most important factor for energy independence in the long term. America's strengths in technology yielded great strides in improving the efficiency of the major energy consumers including automobiles, appliances, heating and cooling systems, and there was finally a commitment to vastly expand mass transportation. Project Energy Independence was declared a success by the end of the decade. America could no longer be threatened by an oil embargo from the Middle East or OPEC. It felt good to be able tell the Arab oil ministers that they could "go pound sand"! OPEC oil would eventually go begging, destroying the economies and political structures in many of the Arab countries.

America had also developed a dependence on "foreign goods" of all types. Unlike many other countries, America always had the natural resources and capabilities to produce these goods, but over the years let economics and global trade take control of the supply chain. The time had come to reduce these dependencies and rebuild America's ability to provide for itself. Agriculture was one of the most important areas that required attention. Although America's heritage was as an agricultural society and at one point the showcase for the world, it had become inefficient and dependent. Small farmers could not compete with large corporate farms. Large farmers were subsidized to prevent overproduction. Imports from less developed countries were cheaper. However, agriculture was still a major export commodity for the United States. America decided to balance its production to its needs, at least within the American continents. Domestic requirements compensated for reduced exports and farms no longer needed subsidies. At the same time, America redeveloped its aquaculture to take advantage of its natural resources and technology. Why should America have to import fish? Aggressive investment and political conviction overcame the artificial barriers of the past and America was once again in control of its own food supply.

Since the Industrial Revolution of the 19th century, America grew proud of its achievements in the production of durables and manufactured goods, but the emergence of low cost labor markets and new industrialized nations moved many jobs and products offshore. This became a major dependency as well as a serious trade deficit. It was time to restore America's pre-eminence in the production of goods, as well as crops. Imports threatened national security in relation to key, critical materials such as steel, precision manufactured goods, and industrial parts. The "high tech" industries were ready to expand once the economic incentives were there. A resurgence in American manufacturing and basic industries, such as mining, oil, and metals took a little longer. It was time to return key industries to the US that had migrated offshore over the years, including the mundane like textiles and clothing, as well as the pervasive electronics. By rebuilding the manufacturing infrastructure in all of the Americas, especially South America, the hemisphere became self sufficient and economically much stronger. It no longer made sense to outsource jobs to the Far East and Africa.

One area of controversy was the production and sale of defense equipment. This was thought to be a major stronghold of US industrial power in the world. America certainly developed and built the most advanced defense technologies. Aerospace and military equipment had traditionally led all categories of exports from the USA, but when it was examined carefully, even this area offered no true advantage to US industry. Major overseas contracts for defense equipment were tied to "offset" packages. These were direct and indirect subsidies to the governments and local industries of the importing countries. Many actually exceeded 100% of the purchase! In addition, the US was often shipping jobs and technology overseas. From a security viewpoint, this had to stop, but self sufficiency and independence in defense equipment turned out to make sense economically as well.

For America to be independent there would have to be significant changes in its trade relations. New trade barriers and tariffs were phased in to protect American markets and support self sufficiency. Since Canada and Mexico were already the largest trading partners with the US, there was a good base to start with to establish a "free trade zone" and self sufficient economy within the Americas. The trade business became a lot easier and more predictable when there were no more inconsistencies, inequities, instabilities and disputes due to trade barriers, such as tariffs, subsidies and embargos. The Rest Of the World would have to find its own solutions.

The financing of the "Fortress" involved some significant economic challenges, including the drastic reductions that had to be made in government programs that were considered "non-strategic." The new independence in resources, goods and crops had dramatic implications for currency, trade and the international stock market. Federal and industry spending caused deficits and recession. Regulation increased to assure more safety and security. Backup controls were established in critical industries including communications, finance, transportation, and energy. Costs of disaster response, counterattacks, rebuilding and security were enormous. There was a great deal of disruption of the global economy while America protected and stabilized itself. This was the end to "Globalization". Initially, it made the protesters and liberal social scientists happy! There would be no more "US cultural imperialism" that had been blamed for the integration of societies and economies. America was now truly independent—and the Rest Of the World would have to live with that.

## VALUES

America had always prided itself on its value system. It was the world's greatest democracy with unequaled individual freedoms; however, it was a very diverse society with no uniform culture or heritage. This was a strength, but perhaps also a weakness. There was crime, poverty, discrimination, immorality, drugs and all the modern social evils. The experiences of 911 and the aftermath led to a wakeup call for America as a society. Terrorism had created a level of anxiety that approached paranoia and panic. For its survival, America had to change. It would need to be stronger if it was to be secure and independent. This realization caused a re-examination of basic American values, and led to a new cultural revolution driven by patriotism and unity.

The United States was widely criticized from within as well as internationally for its tolerance of discrimination, particularly against Blacks and Hispanics. America suddenly realized that they are not the problem. Fundamentalist Islam and the radical and militant cults of all types are! This national reaction led to a war against "fundamentalism", in every form, not just Islam. It included radical "cults" such as white supremacists, religious and racial fanatics, and even fundamentalist Christians and Jews. America sought the end of extremism and radicalism in its society. There was a movement to the mainstream that sought the common denominators of faith and moral values, with no extremes. This new "centrist movement" was building a society at the center of the value system, for security and stability. It was like the fights against Fascism and Communism. America had to ultimately eliminate or isolate terrorism, and the radical fundamentalism that drove it.

The value system that emerged was something like "squeaky clean". It developed a zero tolerance morality and rule of law. There was a major crackdown on crimes of violence, crimes with victims and lesser social crimes such as fraud and corruption. Americans desperately wanted safety and security, so terrorists and criminals were both the enemy. There was even a new emphasis on quality of life law enforcement, as had been successful in New York City. This time, the "War on Crime" was taken seriously.

There also emerged a "Now Generation". Life had new priorities. People didn't have time to fool around with drugs. A new era of self indulgence led to more travel and vacations, but only in America. Early retirement became commonplace. And then came the babies! The increased emphasis on faith and family resulted in the largest baby boom in more than 50 years. People now placed more value and importance on life and happiness. Life had been proven to be too fragile and vulnerable to waste. The trauma of 911 changed attitudes. More people began to take time to care and be nice to each other. There was always a broad base of volunteer activities and organizations in America, but this new level of interest in the welfare of others developed into a major movement of volunteerism. This evolved naturally from the outpouring of sympathy and help from all quarters in response to the 911 attacks, and the subsequent Reign of Terror. There was no reason to let victims or the unfortunate continue to suffer. They were all part of the new America that had to help each other. Social welfare was not a political topic or a government role; it was a moral imperative for all people to deal with. People should not have to be dependent on bureaucratic government agencies for basic needs, when local groups could probably do a better job. Both religious and non-sectarian groups found a vastly expanded and highly motivated resource from the new American value system. In addition to growth in the traditional private sector groups, national programs were launched with government sponsorship and support. When there was no longer an international role for the Peace Corps, the Americorps program expanded dramatically.

This focus on improving values was also felt in religion. There was a resurgence in organized, mainstream religion. This renewal in faith as a driving force in the American way of life reversed the trend of declining attendance and membership in organized religion. Both the Christian and Jewish religions moved quickly to eliminate their extreme fundamentalist groups. Protestant sects, realizing that they still had fundamentally similar values, finally re-consolidated. In a series of what were considered radical moves, the American Catholic Church broke away from the control of the Vatican in Rome. It was then free to merge with its Protestant clone, the Episcopal Church, and then re-unite with the Lutherans. Eventually there emerged a new "American religion" that was ecumenical and non-denominational. This new religion gave new meaning to "God Bless America".

America was known as the "melting pot" of the world. For generations, the country was built and populated by people who had migrated from all regions of the earth. Almost 90% of the recent immigration into the USA was non-European, which began to overwhelm the traditional cultural base of America's heritage. This multi-cultural society was an important part of America's uniqueness, but it became time to amalgamate what it had. There was to be no more "dilution". This was at first very controversial. A closed American society was contrary to the nation's heritage, but it was still the most diverse population in the world. There were plenty of people in all of the major ethnic groups to assure a balance, and ultimately an evolution of the social and cultural characteristics of America. The demographics of the country changed significantly, as much of the population moved away from the target zones of the large US cities. The population was more dispersed as the urban and rural lifestyles began to blend.

Of course, all revolutions cause some dilemmas. America had created a "Freedom Conflict". There would have to be some trade-offs and sacrifice to achieve unity with this new American value system. Security and harmony were not tolerant of the extremes. There was no room for paramilitary and hate groups, no tolerance for fundamentalist religions and "cults", and no sympathy for the support systems for crime and violence, including the drug underworld and the gun lobby. Most felt, even at the beginning, that this was not a bad thing. It would just be difficult to administer fairly and consistently. The pendulum of justice swung firmly towards law and order as the priority of the land. Only those that deserved to be free were entitled to America's freedoms!

# THE FORTRESS PLAN

## ISOLATION

While America was fighting the war on terrorism, it continued to examine its objectives and options. Outwardly, the Administration was united in its resolve and direction, with overwhelming support from Congress and the People. Behind the scenes, however, there was a struggle for consensus. What started as a top-secret debate within the National Security Council after 911, evolved into a high security strategy and ultimately the secret Plan. The failures of Operation "Enduring Freedom" led to support for the extreme measures of the "Fortress America" Plan. The essence of the plan was isolation for security. Many in the leadership believed that no matter how long and hard the country fought terrorism, it could not adequately protect itself as an open society. Only by building the Fortress could America assure peace and safety for future generations. It would have to abandon its traditional international partnerships and relationships, starting with the Middle East. The sympathies and support of terrorists and anti-Americanism of "allies" and "neutral" countries, along with people in the Middle East convinced many that there was no hope for enduring relationships with Egypt, Palestine, and Saudi Arabia. When Israel betrayed America, its long time protector, the US began to abandon its support of Israel. Israel had criticized and refused support to the USA for trying to "appease" the Arabs by forming a coalition with them against terrorism.

It then refused to withdraw from its attacks on the occupied Palestinian territories during the second Intifada. The Israeli destruction of the Jenin refugee camp under the premise of hunting terrorists resulted in hundreds of casualties and the loss of support of many Allied nations. It also increased the intensity of hatred by Arabs, and created a new source of suicide bombers and terrorists. These actions proved to be a tragic mistake and historical error on the part of Israel.

The Palestinian War gave the Fortress America Plan a sense of urgency and broadened its base of support within the Administration. Relations between the Palestinian leadership and Israel broke down and then off completely. This led to an escalation of terrorist attacks on Israel and retaliation by Israel on Palestinian territories. Israel struck out with force at areas suspected to be the sources of Palestinian terrorists. How could they, though, isolate the enemy from the civilian population? The casualties were high and the damage extensive. More terrorism and riots followed. Marshall Law was imposed. Eventually the war came; first within the Palestinian territories, and then with neighboring Arab states—again! The ten year cycle continued. This time, though, the United States decided not to intercede. The long history of unfaltering support for Israel was eroded by America's disenchantment with the Middle East. It was time for America to begin to look out for itself. The war on terrorism had taken its toll. The United States lost its motivation to be the policeman for the world. Security of the Homeland took priority.

The nuclear terrorist attack on Israel was *the last straw*. Israel retaliated with all of its military force, targeting all of the neighboring Arab countries. This was followed by a resurgence of militant Islamic groups and terrorist organizations throughout Islamic states. America was forced to abandon its strategic military bases in Islamic countries including Saudi Arabia, Kuwait, Afghanistan, Pakistan, and Uzbekistan.

All US military forces were pulled back to safe harbors. All US personnel, government and civilian, were removed from the region; from all
countries in the Middle East, Southwest Asia and all Muslim countries.
The Fortress America Plan was being implemented.


## THE OFFENSE

The most controversial part of the Plan was the next step, which was
critical to America's isolation and protection. It was time to deploy the
ultimate offense; to stop the terror long enough for America to withdraw into its Fortress. There had been several years of hot debates
behind the closed doors of the National Security leadership, followed by
years of preparation. All of the security and military agencies had to be
involved. The investments that had been made in building America's
defense systems and independent resources were an integral part of The
Plan, and it would need to unify the support of its political partnerships
in the Western Hemisphere as it pulled back its military and diplomatic
presence from the Rest Of the World.

What military strategy could assure success this time? Ground force
invasions were proven to be impractical. There was no support from
neighboring countries. America's "allies" were not motivated to pursue
a major offensive or provide access to air and ground bases in the
Persian Gulf as they had in the past. There was also a risk of high casualties. The Top Secret military plan was called "Operation Parking Lot".
It had been in preparation for years; identifying targets, planning
attacks, and exploring options. Its objective was to devastate the most
intransigent strongholds of global terrorism and anti-Americanism.
This was intended to be the last strike at the enemy before isolating
America from the world it could no longer trust or tolerate. The
"hawks" in the Administration had advocated extreme measures almost

from the beginning of the Reign of Terror. They wanted to make "parking lots" out of all the countries that nurtured and harbored the enemy. As the terror continued, and the violence in the Middle East escalated, their views gained support and serious planning began. How would the targets, though, be chosen? Which regions were destined to become "parking lots"? Who would decide, and how would America live with that decision? It was not easy and involved enormous risk. Once deployed, this military operation would leave America no choice but to abandon the world it had known, and change it forever.

The "hawks" ultimately had to compromise (a little). Operation Parking Lot was not implemented with the full scope in which it was originally imagined, but it was still devastating. The American leaders recognized the realities of civilized behavior and the responsibilities of a world leader, even one that had been attacked and betrayed. The decision was made to choose three "parking lots". This was not to be an attack on the "Axis of Evil". It would be tactical and focused on the most persistent US enemies and terrorist threats. Iraq was the easiest and first choice. There were a lot of reasons. The obvious immediate justification was retaliation for supporting the nuclear attack on Israel. In addition, there were all the years of harboring and supporting terrorist organizations, and Iraq's unforgivable acts of aggression. They never showed remorse for their invasion of Kuwait, or for killing their own people in the nerve gas attack on the Kurdish town of Halabja in 1988, where 5000 died and many thousands were injured with long term effects. The real threat was the development of weapons of mass destruction together with their Scud missiles as a delivery system. This ruled out a ground invasion because of the potential for high casualties from biological and chemical weapons attacks. Of course, there was always the desire to rid the world of the renegade warlord Saddam Hussein. It was decided to destroy all known Iraqi military installations, facilities capable of developing and storing weapons of mass destruction, hideouts and headquarters of terrorist groups, and finally, all known facilities to house Saddam Hussein and his leadership.

The second target was another thorn that had stuck in the side of America for decades—Libya. The time was long overdue for retribution for the bombing of Pan Am flight 103 that killed 270 innocent American and British citizens in 1988. A lone Libyan Intelligence Officer was convicted, but the Libyan government had remained defiant. It was also time to punish Libya's support and harboring of terrorist groups. There was also the incorrigible Muammar Qadhafi. The US plan was to destroy all known Libyan military installations, facilities capable of developing and storing weapons of mass destruction, hideouts and headquarters of terrorist groups, and facilities to house Muammar Qadhafi and his leadership. The two most infamous terrorist states and their renegade leaders would finally be put out of business.

The third target was more controversial. The United States had supported Afghanistan through two wars of independence. But now was the time to punish Afghanistan for its betrayal of America. The resurgence of militant Islamic groups and hatred of America raised a whole new generation of potential terrorists. Afghanistan had returned to its roots as a home for smuggling, corruption, and lawlessness. It was a country run by ruthless warlords and thieves; not a nation, but a renegade haven. After the war, there was rebuilding of the terrorist camps and harboring of known terrorists. This region was hopeless. However, it had been decimated during decades of war, so the targets were few. All of the new military installations would be destroyed, taking away, once again, the power base of the corrupt warlord society. The major cave complexes and mountain passes would be destroyed to remove the traditional terrorist hideouts and escape routes forever. The tough but necessary decision was to devastate the region of Islamic extremists along the southeastern border with Pakistan, which had been the source of the Taliban and the safe harbor for al Qaeda. The "tribal areas" bridged the border between both Afghanistan and Pakistan, but were never really under the control of either country. Since millions of people lived in this region, there would be many civilian casualties, but America learned the hard way that it could not distinguish the innocent, allies or enemies in this region. And finally, the poppy fields of Helmand Province would be destroyed forever. Since Afghanistan supplied 75% of the world's opium and heroin, this would severely disrupt the global drug trade, and in turn, deter a major cause of crime.

Other targets were considered, including the Sudan, Yemen, and North Korea. The rationale and commitment was not as strong. So, the line was drawn around the three targets and preparations were made for Operation Parking Lot. A variety of military alternatives were considered. The United States had a vast arsenal of weapons at its disposal. It could either use precision bombing on specific targets, or mass bombing for maximum destruction. There was also high impact bombing that could be used for "bunker busting". Then there were nuclear weapons that could be used to destroy major key areas and installations such as underground facilities, military installations, terrorist headquarters and camps—to render them unusable forever. However, the question of how to avoid civilian concentration areas was asked.

The debates over this plan were long and difficult, but a rationale emerged that sold all of the American leadership, and ultimately the public. America had to be unified on this action to move forward as a nation. It could not afford to second guess such a fateful decision. There was no looking back. Collectively, the reasons were compelling. This was not a military decision. It was an historic decision about the survival of a society. America had chosen to devastate its enemies and withdraw to protective isolation.

Of course, this would be seen by the world as retaliation for the latest attacks on the US and Israel. It was the last straw in challenging the patience of America's military power. That was, though, a simplistic view of what was a heated debate and comprehensive assessment of the situation and the prospects. If left unchecked, the terror could continue like Ireland and Israel, for years, institutionalized as a way of life. This was unacceptable to Americans who valued life, freedom and peace. The US found that it could not "weed out" all the terrorists, and it couldn't stop the creation and training of new terrorists. It was not able to win "the hearts and minds" of the people of the terrorist and Islamic extremist states. International sanctions did not isolate these states effectively. Their populaces were hopelessly indoctrinated with hate of United States.

But what about innocent civilians? How could the US rationalize the inevitable impact of such a major offensive? These countries offered no redeeming values or hope for the future. Militant Muslims, especially the Taliban, Iraqis, and Libyans, routinely put their populations at risk by moving military personnel into general civilian locations. It wasn't possible to separate targets. Besides, the "women and children" may also be terrorist risks. Many had willingly joined in terrorist attacks, even suicide missions. Why should the USA try to avoid or spare so-called "innocent civilians" in a country we are at war with? What about the thousands of innocent Americans who were casualties of the 911 terrorist attacks and the aftermath of the secondary attacks? Besides, the people of these countries were already destined to poverty, hardship, oppression, and early death. A harsh, but actuarial rationalization.

Afghanistan had been constantly at war for more than 20 years, so what was "salvageable"? It had large areas of buried mines; many thousands, maybe even millions that endangered all that lived there. Afghanistan had a history of tribal and foreign wars for 700 years. The country was in a hopelessly endless state of conflict. The Taliban had persecuted and massacred thousands of Hazaras, the Shiite minority. After the war, regional fighting broke out between ethnic groups. There was retaliation for past abuses and atrocities. The Northern Tajiks and Uzbeks fought the Pashtuns that were a majority in the South, but a minority in the North. Rape, murder and pillage were rampant. It was "medieval". The life expectancy in Afghanistan was very low. The average for men was about 44. At the same time, the high birth rate created a proliferation of future Islamic fundamentalists. Women were subjugated. Polygamy was commonplace. There was no infrastructure. It had no roads or utilities. Afghanistan returned to being the world's largest producer of opium, the source of heroin, which was refined in Pakistan. Opium was the major cash crop. Nothing else yielded more money or was as easy to grow. Afghanistan and Pakistan relied heavily on smuggling and drug traffic; with Taliban support and "taxes". In Afghanistan, there would be no "collateral damage"!

The American people grew impatient for retribution and resolution. They wanted to avoid a "quagmire" like Vietnam had been. The "hawks" finally prevailed. Only total annihilation of the terrorist states would be effective in dismantling and eliminating the networks and threats. Conventional bombing only blew up empty buildings, caves and rocks. How could America drop nuclear weapons on the civilian population of other countries? Unfortunately, it was not like it was unprecedented. After all, the US was the only country to have ever done it before when it devastated the cities of Hiroshima and Nagasaki to end the war with Japan in 1945. Together with the fire bombing of Tokyo that preceded the atom bombs, there were hundreds of thousands of deaths and casualties.

The missiles were fired almost simultaneously, with satellite control and surveillance. Each was equipped with nuclear warheads to yield the total devastation of the targets being attacked. The latest generation of nuclear weapons was capable of penetrating and destroying deep underground facilities—not just the caves and hideouts of terrorists, but the secret "factories" for weapons of mass destruction. The high intensity and heat from these missiles would destroy the chemical, biological and nuclear stockpiles. Areas with large concentrations of the leadership and military were also specifically targeted, but inevitably there was substantial "collateral damage". America provided a last minute top secret alert to its allies at the time, including Russia. There was no going back. The gates of the Fortress were being closed.

## THE FEDERATION

While the United States was fighting the war on terrorism, it was also preparing itself for the isolation that would come as a result of its defensive and offensive strategies. The strict security measures and the impact of its retaliation would make its traditional relationships with the world impractical. The United States, however, did not have to "go it alone". It had natural allies and partners for the long term. Although it was not practical for the USA to close its borders with Canada and Mexico, it was possible to purge North America and control its natural borders. It could build a new and stronger America. So it started a transition that had already begun to evolve from the United States of America to a federation of the Americas.

The United States decided that it was not worth the price, in terms of costs and risks, and sacrifice in terms of the ultimate loss of life and assets, and the hatred of the Third World, to be the world's policeman, protector, benefactor and babysitter! After 50 years of unsatisfying and unfinished wars, the USA decided to withdraw from its global leadership role. The terrorist attacks of 2001 followed years of regional conflicts of a "horrific" nature and an unrelenting "quagmire" of conflict, including the Middle East, Africa, and the Balkans, as well as an increasing and widespread number of what appeared to be isolated terrorist incidents worldwide. The Fortress strategy was for the isolation of the Americas by a union of the countries of North and South America—The American Federation.

For this to work, the US needed to make an attractive "deal" with the other American countries. External security was, of course, a major factor. The USA could offer the world's strongest defense and military protection. At the same time, the natural borders of the Western Hemisphere would lend themselves to a more cohesive and comprehensive defense. This American Federation would also provide economic opportunity for all the countries involved. After all, it represented a major portion of the developed world. The agreements and processes between countries could be simplified. Open trade, together with the economic development support of the USA, would provide stimulation and growth for the region. The American Federation could survive independently by the exploitation of its vast resources including energy, materials, and agriculture as well as a broad-based manufacturing infrastructure. The US would also be a critical source of technology support and development to provide for continued economic strength in the future. Open borders would facilitate the immigration, jobs, trade, and tourism necessary to sustain a strong economy within the Federation.

There were even some important secondary benefits. The inevitable cultural and language integration would lead to a bilingual and more heterogeneous America. The Hispanic population had already become the largest and fastest growing minority group in the United States. So, joining with Latin America was not a radical departure from the existing demographic trends. And the tough US law enforcement would eventually eliminate drugs and violent crime. In fact, the Federation would step up to solve a number of serious chronic problems, such as the poverty in Mexico, the drug infrastructure in Columbia, and the financial instability in Argentina. For the Federation to work, in practical terms, it had to maintain internal political autonomy for each of the countries. It also required strict internal security requirements with the support of the "Fortress network". The external security and military were unified, including controlled borders of the overall Federation.

The American Federation was originally built on the Organization of American States as well as the increasingly stronger ties of the United States to Canada and Mexico. It then rapidly accelerated into a more formal relationship as security and economic independence became a common cause for survival. There were naturally strong economic and social ties between these countries. They already shared a great deal in trade, industry and resources. It was not unrealistic to drive for self-sufficiency. The countries of Latin America were committed to the Federation, but their full assimilation would have to be a long term process. After the US took the dramatic offensive actions against the terrorist states the other "Americas" were anxious to unite for common military and economic security. It would start as a loose federation, more like a combination of the UN, NATO and GATT, and then evolve over time.

The decision to unite the Americas was very difficult. The challenges would be enormous; economical, military and cultural difficulties in particular. The Fortress, though, had to have secure walls. The price would be to clean up the poverty, crime and corruption of the Central and South American countries. They had to bear the primary responsibility, but would have the economic and military protection of the Federation. Each country would have to earn its "membership" in the Federation by showing progress in political reform and public security. They all had there own internal terrorist challenges. Peru had the communist insurgents of the "Shining Path". Columbia was in the worst shape. It had a variety of competing groups that terrorized the nation: the Revolutionary Armed Forces of Columbia (FARC); the National Liberation Army (ELN); and the United Self Defense Forces of Columbia (AUC). These were rebels, guerrillas and paramilitary organizations that kidnapped and killed at will with the support of the drug trade. Of course, the differences between these lawless regions of Latin America and the USA had diminished during the Reign of Terror. The security problem was basically the same, and so would be the solutions. It would take decades to accomplish, and would need the help of some "mop up" operations from the Federation military forces to clean out the strongest guerilla groups. When it was done, though, it would all be part of America, not some remote foreign state with an uncertain future. All Americans had a vested interest in the success of unification. The new America would be stronger.

When the Federation was able to demonstrate viability, it expanded. The Caribbean Republic was formed among all the island nations, including Cuba, the Bahamas, and Bermuda. Havana became the seat of government and San Juan took the leadership as the business, finance and cultural center. As the Western Hemisphere grew secure in its isolation, Australia and New Zealand were compelled to join the Federation. After all, Australia and New Zealand, along with Canada, provided military support to the war on terrorism, as they had in the past wars fought with the leadership of the USA. They also shared a similar cultural heritage. Together with Hawaii and the Pacific island possessions, the security fence of the American Federation now spans more than halfway around the earth. The US finally provided nation status to all of its territories and possessions.

How could the Federation have formed so quickly? It actually took years, it evolved over time, and it was facilitated by increasing ties and interdependencies with the US as it built its plan for independence. The need for a strong American Federation was triggered by the offensive attacks. Countries were highly motivated to join by the attraction of the American defense and protection as well as the prospect of economic strength and reform. It was a natural assimilation and rationalization of realities.

The United States, followed by the other countries in the new American Federation, withdrew from NATO and the UN. They now had to focus on protecting their own world. The UN facilities in New York were closed and turned into prime commercial real estate. The American Federation was now secure. After ten years of hard work, sacrifice and difficult decisions, it was at last a reality. Fortress America would survive. It was isolated, but it was strong. It was purged and was now impenetrable. The American Federation was a democracy, but it was a very controlled. It was a Fortress state—now alone in a world of its own.

## ROW

So what was to happen with the Rest Of the World when America withdrew from its world leadership role? Europe, Asia, the Middle East and Africa were left to survive on their own. Without the USA as the world's policeman, wars broke out between long-standing feuding countries: India and Pakistan, Japan and Korea, China and Taiwan, and of course, Israel and the Arab States. With no political, military or economic pressure from the US, the historical ethnic wars persisted in the Balkan and African regions. Some states dominated; the European Union and China in particular. Europe had its own self interest and needs. It could not share the same level of commitment to the war on terrorism as America. Some did not even sympathize with the objectives. Europe had a fragmented and divergent social and political heritage from America and had to strengthen the ties established within the EU to survive as a regional confederation. South Africa became the sole economic power of its continent that was otherwise a hopeless disaster.

The political map of the world changed dramatically. Impoverished countries went without help. Most were taken over by tyrannical rulers and others were conquered. Some just "died". Russia stayed independent of the former Soviet Union states, especially Muslim countries, and gave up the remaining ones—Chechnya, Tartarstan, and Dagestan. Russia eventually joined with Europe, and together with the Eastern European States, formed the Eurasian Confederation, which in some regards replaced NATO, as well as the European Union. The Organization of the Islamic Conference had a much broader representation and appeal than the Arab League. It was comprised of 50 Muslim countries, and formed the foundation for establishing an "Islamic Confederation". It joined politically and economically with countries from Africa to South West Asia to Indonesia, many of which were contiguous. The more developed Muslim countries took the lead in the confederation; Malaysia, Turkey and Tunisia, but they suffered a "Brain Drain". The Middle East had already lost many of their best and brightest. Many successful, educated professionals had already left Iran, Egypt and Saudi Arabia to work and live in the US and Europe. The Islamic Confederation had no allies. It was isolated from the rest of the world by its culture and violent history. Now it would have to survive on its own, and try not to self destruct from old internal conflicts.

Over time, it became natural to form other regional ethnic confederations. To overcome their long history of border wars and power struggles, the Oriental Confederation was formed comprising China, South

East Asia, Mongolia, Japan and Korea. The economic and military incentives were stronger than their traditional conflicts, and their cultural and language heritage would provide a natural bond. This one was going to be able to work. Some of these confederations made treaties on peace and trade with the American Federation, but no mutual defense or weapons restrictions were established.

And as for Israel, the decades of conflict with the Palestinians and neighboring Arab countries finally took its toll. The wars and retaliations that killed so many civilians created an entire generation of Arabs that would always hate Israel. Of course, the terrorized Israelis felt the same way about the Arabs. There was no longer hope for reconciliation, co-existence or peace. And Israel had to react quickly to the withdrawal of US support. Israel had to either eliminate the Palestinians or give up their territories. It could no longer defend itself against its internal or external enemies. So, it gave up the land and population of the Palestinians. Israel was used to making sacrifices for security. Separating the Palestinians was long overdue and not really the problem. There were one million Palestinian Arabs who were Israeli citizens in addition to the 2 ½ million living in occupied territories. It had to abandon the Israeli settlements in conquered and annexed territories. Israel transferred back Gaza to Egypt, the West Bank to Jordan, and the Golan Heights to Syria, returning to its 1967 borders. All Arabs, even Israeli citizens, were expelled from Israel. And all Israelis left the Palestinian territories. This was not an easy task. It was a major relocation program and very unpleasant for those Israeli "pioneers" who settled in the long disputed Palestinian territories. There were more than 200,000 Israelis scattered in over 160 settlements in the West Bank and Gaza. It also proved to be a mixed blessing for the Palestinians. In addition to the million Israeli Arabs who were expelled from Israel, there were more than two million Palestinians who had been living in refugee camps in Syria, Jordan, and Lebanon that had to return to their new homeland.

Moving millions of people across the borders of this small region was a traumatic and difficult process.

The new borders were closed. Israel built a wall around itself, literally, to keep Palestinians out and Israelis in. It was an armed and fortified wall more imposing and advanced than what had worked for East Germany. Jerusalem, like Berlin, was divided by the Wall. There was an extensive network of border guards, security monitors and a strong air defense system. The "Wall of Separation" used a variety of advanced technologies, such as motion sensors and night vision, in addition to a combination of conventional methods including watch towers, mine fields, and fences. Israel became a fortress state unto itself; always under siege, but no longer from within. It was reduced to a small isolated country, with no allies, in the midst of a bitter Arab world. Five million Jews were surrounded by 250 million Arabs. Israel was left to sustain itself—as it had for over 5000 years!

There were no winners in this new world order. Some of the new confederations would be strong, but some regions would be losers; especially Africa, the Asian subcontinent, and the Middle East. Most of the Rest Of the World was hopelessly impoverished and at war. Many countries were ruled by tyrants and hated America. With no US support or bail out, weak economies faltered. Recession spread worldwide. Chaos was rampant. The new world order—was disorder!

# THE LOSSES

America invested a decade in fighting terrorism and building the Fortress. It succeeded in implementing its strategy for survival, and its people would be safe and secure, but it came at a great price. The losses would have major historical ramifications. However, the average law biding, tax paying, god loving citizen did not feel that they lost something significant with the new America that brought them the security in their lives that they now treasure so much.

There were some very significant missed opportunities. If the United States persevered in building a coalition against terrorism, it could have been an opportunity to unite the world for peace. And there was an opportunity to revitalize Central Asia rather than destroy and abandon it. Just think what it would have been like with democracy, trade, healthcare and women's rights. Not to mention the great potential for developing oil and gas resources.

America also compromised some of its own values and objectives. It relaxed environmental regulations and restrictions to facilitate energy exploration and distribution. It sacrificed privacy and personal freedoms for the sake of security. It could be argued that some of the values and laws now approach some of the extremes of the fundamentalist Islam it denounced.

Even the Military lost. The United States had the best prepared military force in the world. It was the most practiced by fighting regular wars of its own and others for over 100 years! Within the Fortress, it will lose "practice" and readiness. Maybe that is not a bad price to pay for security.

The greatest price, though, was the loss of freedom and opportunity for mankind. America let a bunch of "crazies" change the history of the world and reduce the potential of a "great society" in the United States. Americans rallied after 911 and proclaimed that "they can't take our freedom away". And yet, in the end, they did! When the President of the United States declared on the eve of the 911 attacks that America was the "brightest beacon for freedom and opportunity in the world", he could not have realized that it would ultimately be extinguished by its own acts!

Fortress America is strong—but it lost its destiny for greatness.

# Afterword

This is a retrospective looking back on 911 as a historical landmark that created a point of departure and change for the world as we knew it. It is not a desired or necessarily correct outcome of the reality that followed the fateful events of 911. However, it is a possibility. Events can change history and civilization dramatically—and not necessarily for the better. This is an extremely critical period for the United States and the world. The temptations for emotional reactions and quick solutions will be great. America took over 200 years to build its principles and pursue its destiny—but could lose its direction in just a few years.

**God bless—and God help—America.**

# About the Author

Henry P. Mitchell is a writer publishing under a pen name to protect his privacy and security. He is proud to be an American, but very concerned about the nation's future.

0-595-23522-0